CRUISE CONTROL

CRUISE CONTROL

by

Victoria Jenkins

For Vales —
All best wishes —
Victoria Jenkins

THE PERMANENT PRESS
SAG HARBOR, NY 11963

Library of Congress Cataloging-in-Publication Data

Jenkins, Victoria
    Cruise Control /by Victoria Jenkins
      p. cm.
    ISBN 1-57962-045-0 (alk paper)
    1. Hollywood (Los Angeles, Calif)--Fiction. 2. Women screen
    writers--Fiction. 3. Northwest, Pacific--Fiction.
    4. Single mothers--Fiction. 5. Adultery--Fiction. I. Title

    PS3560.E514 C78 2002
    813'.54--dc21   2001036614
                                      CIP

Printed in the United States of America

THE PERMANENT PRESS
4170 Noyac Road
Sag Harbor, NY 11963

Acknowledgements

I am indebted to many friends for careful reading, thoughtful criticism and encouragement, especially: Connie Poten, Peter Stark and Bill Vaughn. Thanks to the Rattlesnake Ladies Salon. And thanks also to Kate Mulgrew and to Bob Bergman.

For My Boys

And In Memory of My Mother

One

THE DAY HER husband filed divorce papers Louise bought a pair of red pumps with open toes and four-inch heels and wore them out of the store. She hadn't gone looking for shoes or gone shopping at all, she was just wandering while her life took a turn at someone else's hands. That's the way she thought of it, like a tilt in pinball, as though she had nothing to do with it.

The shoes were a complete departure, nothing she'd ever have considered formerly. Later she made an association with Dorothy and Oz and the ruby slippers, but she wasn't thinking of that at the time. She wrote a check from the joint account so they'd be a present from her husband — shoes from him for her to walk in as she departed the known universe.

Outside, things looked sharply focused and distant as though she'd stretched and was looking at the world from a great height. A building was going up on the other side of the street. Louise couldn't remember what had been there before. A parking lot maybe, or an Army Navy store. She wasn't sure where she was. Kidnapped by aliens and returned to the wrong location, the wrong city, the wrong body or with some key chip excised. She didn't feel anything like herself. She had no idea which direction to turn, no recollection of where she'd parked the car.

She stood outside the shoe shop and watched a workman at the construction site carry a sheet of plywood across an I-beam three stories up. He walked like a runway model, his feet winging out and coming down directly in line with each other.

Once, while she was watching, a Japanese dancer had fallen to the pavement between buildings during an aerial performance above the streets of downtown. A rope gave way

9

and he plummeted like a stone. In the perfect silence that accompanied his fall she heard him hit with a sound like a melon in a sack.

Now Louise held her breath until the workman reached a platform and dropped the plywood. It landed with a *whumpf* she could hear from where she stood. He looked down and saw her watching.

His performance was like the dancer's, only executed successfully and incidentally in the course of his everyday work, which Louise admired. She wanted to applaud, but was afraid of what he'd think. She wasn't one of those easy, friendly girls lavish with good will, though she wished she were and part of the time she felt she could train herself to be.

She adopted his gait as she walked away, teetering in the high heels, her hips rocking, and she heard him whistle behind her. That hadn't happened for a while. She turned around. He waved, but her arm didn't want to lift in return. Maybe from his vantage she looked cheery, but she was suddenly trying not to cry.

Her husband was still in the house when she came home, though he'd agreed to be out, gone. She looked down on him as she walked past, taller than he in the pumps. She'd always been careful not to do that. She'd worn flats on his account. He didn't say anything, but he took it in with a baffled expression transparent as a window. She could see the wheels turn. He was processing the unwelcome information that he might have been patronized all this time, his ego catered to. And it was supposed to be her job to shield him from such wounding revelations: a double whammy.

He was absolutely familiar — her familiar for almost twenty years — transformed overnight into a stranger as though aliens had been monkeying with *him*.

She could have made him laugh if she'd wanted, struck a pose or said something that would have turned the shoes into a joke or a disguise and turned her back into herself in order to console him, but she didn't. She didn't trust him anymore. He would misinterpret anything she said or did and take it as an effort to win him back and use it against her if he could. They were operating under a new protocol now and she had to watch herself.

She stalked into the kitchen where the counters were suddenly too low and she could see dust on top of the refrigerator she hadn't known was there. He didn't follow her, but left the house without saying anything. Walked out, heavy-footed on the porch steps: Elliot, her husband, who announced every departure and kissed her at the door and told her where he was headed each time he left the room, even if it was only to go upstairs to the bathroom. They were like Siamese twins who shared organs, and when he left he took something essential to her function. She didn't know how she would manage without him. It would be like surviving without a liver.

Vast blocks of time evaporated, leaving no memory. Louise supposed she did the normal things, that she wrote at her desk — her work — and drove to the market and assembled meals and folded clothes, but she was like an Alzheimer's patient without any short-term memory, though the past was vivid. In their absences, while they were at school or with their father, she pictured her boys as they had been years earlier and was surprised at each homecoming by how they'd grown, as though she'd missed or forgotten a whole stage of development.

She slept all over the house like a cat. She woke at odd hours and prowled through the dark rooms. The night filled the house like a substance, as though darkness poured in each evening, thicker than air, suspending her like salt water. She looked in on the boys and listened to them breathe and touched their foreheads while they slept. And on the Wednesday nights and weekends when they weren't there she sometimes lay down on their beds. She slept on the couch in the living room and in the guest bedroom upstairs. She had gotten very thin and hardly left an impression. She watched the moon from every window, didn't read, and never turned on the television or the lights. Across town her husband was sleeping in his girl-friend's bed. He had never spent a night alone.

Two

SIX MONTHS LATER on a miserable December day the divorce was final. Construction on the bus tunnel had downtown on its ear. Traffic was rerouted and sidewalks closed. Louise had to park blocks away down by the waterfront. It was cold and spitting rain, the air thick and soggy. She made her way up the hill to the Superior Court Building along a plywood arcade where gangs had sprayed hieroglyphics. Heavy equipment operating underground sent tremors through the pavement beneath her feet.

She waited in a crowded basement courtroom to be summoned forward to a glass booth where the magistrate presided to hear the decree read and to sign it. Her husband had signed already on some earlier occasion. It was practical, Louise supposed, not to require the presence of both parties, and only coincidentally humane. She wondered if the glass was bulletproof against the possibility of deranged former spouses.

Louise had dressed for the occasion and looked like one of the lawyers. Normally, she wore jeans. She had thought for a long time about what to wear, standing in front of her closet. She'd been married in a creamy satin dress that her mother sewed for her, inside-out for a matte effect, utterly simple, and slim and short and cut on the bias to minimize the yardage needed. And a lace mantilla dipped in tea. Now she was wearing black. Louise believed that there was little enough in life to celebrate, so it was necessary to memorialize the small stuff, good and bad. Make your own moments. Otherwise her graph would be flat as a cardiac arrest.

A jackhammer outside rattled the windows. She could see the ankles of people passing on the sidewalk, scissoring purposefully along. Places to go, things to do.

An enormous family of many generations, dressed as if for church, squeezed into the room and stood along the wall passing around what seemed to be a Chinese baby. They brought a celebratory air into the judicial setting. "An adoption," Louise's attorney said. "The only happy thing that goes on down here."

The appointed time came and went. Louise's lawyer was on the clock, the meter mounting in six-minute increments. They billed in tenths of hours like the government.

Louise occupied herself with studying the adoption party, trying to figure out who the various people were to each other. She couldn't even put together a plausible set to be the parents. Gays perhaps, or a single-parent adoption. Later, beset by misfortune, someone in that family might look back and remember her, a baleful presence on the periphery of their jubilation like a bad omen.

Afterwards, when the papers were signed and Louise was officially divorced, her attorney proposed a drink, pro forma, pro bono. Louise limply accepted. There was nothing she wanted to talk about, but the court proceeding was anticlimactic, as banal and drearily bureaucratic as renewing her driver's license, and she was still hoping for a ceremonial moment to cap things, some epiphany to provide a line of demarcation.

They went to McCormick's and sat in the bar among the well-suited lunch crowd. Dark wood and black and white tiles provided a more august atmosphere than the carpeted halls of justice they'd just left where pomp had succumbed to utility. Louise ordered champagne and immediately regretted it. The champagne seemed pallid and euphemistic and produced an instant headache and the image of herself in a pastel suit and a pillbox, dotty on kir in the middle of the day without the slightest connection to reality. She wished she'd asked for a belt of something cauterizing, a double gin martini or straight tequila.

After, Louise huddled under the McCormick's awning with her attorney, who was herself divorced and who had had cancer besides and who was hence more unfortunate than she, though Louise wasn't at that moment interested in the inspirational example that might be thus provided. Louise stuck out her hand to avoid the false warmth of an embrace, then they broke cover into the rain and hurried in their own directions. There'd be no call to meet again.

She sat beside the phone through the afternoon but it didn't ring and she didn't call. She was waiting for Richard, the magus who had derailed her life. He knew it was today; she'd told him. It was biblical, Louise thought, like something out of the Old Testament, unlike most of life where there was no apparent correlation between behavior and consequence. She had wanted too much and had been unable to choose between Richard and her husband until they both gave up waiting around for her to decide, simultaneously it seemed, as though attraction vanished when competition did. Now she had neither.

She thought about calling Ingrid, who lived down the street and around the corner and was her best friend, but didn't. At Ingrid's she would obliterate the afternoon with wisecracks and more wine. At home alone she could extend time, stretch out the moment that lay between two segments of her life. As soon as she began talking she would propel herself into her future, redesign herself as a divorcée. Her solitary afternoon was a bridge that grew longer the longer she preserved it, creating a separation between before and after.

With other couples she knew, whose divorces were less rancorous, one former partner might call the other at this

15

moment in tribute to the past. Not hers, though. Hers was celebrating somewhere, toasting "good riddance" with his soon-to-be next wife. And not her either, too jumpy to risk it.

The rain had turned serious and pelted down and the afternoon darkened into evening before the children were home from school. Louise was glad when it was time to turn on the lights and the radio and begin the routine of dinner and homework, which lifted her out of herself and deposited her in her own personal Kansas where things were normal and she felt at home and useful.

That night she moved into the really quite foreign territory of her husband's side of the bed. The lamp and the phone were over there, but she'd continued to sleep neatly on her own side, hardly disturbing the bedclothes, exactly as though he were only out and would be coming home late to slip in beside her.

He'd slept in his underwear like a farmer, his skin white and damp, cool as a mushroom. He'd slept like a rock, never hearing the children call. When they first were married he'd taken the side closest to the door, purportedly a first line of defense against intruders, but it was soon clear that that was a joke — Louise had to jostle him awake if there was ever an alarm in the night. In the tiny house where they'd lived when the boys were born, their bed was against the wall and Louise had clambered over the top of him whenever a baby woke and cried.

Three

LOUISE TOOK THE boys to San Francisco for Christmas, where the chilly grandeur of her father's and stepmother's house inhibited them all, anesthetized them, and where they had to watch their hands and feet and modulate everything in fear of a gaffe.

They negotiated the rituals of the tree and Christmas Eve champagne and the excess of Christmas morning dry-eyed. Then in the interlude between presents and dinner, Louise had to take the boys to the airport for the flight to Seattle, the hand-off to her husband for his half of the vacation. The first of many.

A bomb in a suitcase had exploded somewhere in the world and they wouldn't let her out to the gate to see her children onto the plane but made her say good-bye at the security checkpoint. The boys' faces were pale and strained with anxieties she had caused and now didn't know how to ease. At that moment she would have gladly turned the clock back, endured anything or foregone anything if only she could put their world back together. She thought fleetingly of snatching away their tickets, grabbing their hands, and running for the parking garage where they'd left her father's car. If they made a break for the border they'd be halfway to Mexico before the plane landed in Seattle without the boys and the alarm went out. But she lacked the nerve or the conviction that that was what she really wanted to do, or what they wanted, or that she could carry it off. Perhaps it came down to the same thing. She had her feet planted in cement.

The boys turned around and waved where the concourse turned a corner, then they were gone. The airport was deserted except for a few other fractured families like hers shunting the kids off to the other parent in a barbaric modern Yuletide convention. There was nowhere to wait where she could see the plane and bestow a mental benediction, but she watched the monitor until it announced the plane had lifted off.

The freeway back into town was empty. The trip in from the airport hadn't changed much from her own childhood every-other-Christmas visits. Green hills, blue sky, white city, ruffled bay. She hated it. She hated San Francisco where she was always cold and wanting a bath and hungry for something she couldn't name. It was a holdover from her own days as a child of divorce; never at home here, always a visitor, missing her cat and her mother and the wan and brief observance of the holiday she was used to.

Back at her father's house, in the beautiful circular candle-lit dining room, they ate the Christmas goose, followed as always by a Bûche de Noel from Gumps or Fantasia or some new bakery down on Union, decorated with chocolate bark and marzipan toadstools which her niece and nephews all claimed, though they would find, as she always had, that they tasted grittily medicinal.

The boys telephoned during dessert to say they were back in Seattle and their father wasn't there to meet them and they didn't know where they should wait for him and what was she doing now. Louise hung up and began to cry. There was a butler's pantry off the kitchen, and for the first time in her life, she behaved as if she lived there and went in and found a bottle of brandy and carried it out to the dining room and poured an inch into her empty Sauterne glass.

"Pour me some of that, too," said her brother, always an eager partner in self medication.

Her father got up and fetched appropriate glasses without a word. "Salud," said Louise. Everybody wore somber faces out of deference, but no one met her eyes and Louise felt messy and hopeless. Humpty Dumpty in a family of intact eggs.

Louise slept on the analytic couch in her stepmother's office at the top of the house. Silk walls and a view of the bridge. Years and years of tears in your ears was someone's description of analysis. It seemed unlucky and foolhardy to sleep here where so many people lay down and wrestled their demons—like sleeping in a cemetery. Some people wouldn't do it.

She was awake at five and heard the bugler sound reveille down in the Presidio. In the dark the orchids on the window sill looked like enormous moths against the glass.

Four

NOTHING CHANGED. Louise had thought that in the new year things would be different and she'd start over. But she didn't know what to start over *as.* And no one to consult. Days marched forward uniformly like cards.

In certain small ways that seemed safe and inconsequential she tried to retool. She moved things around in the house and arranged the furniture according to the principles of feng shui, not quite believing that this would alter her luck or create harmony but less confident than before in her habitual skepticism. The ancient Chinese might be right. Maybe the seat of her marital discord lay, in fact, in the location of the kitchen range. Which she couldn't change. But upstairs she swung the bed around so that the axis lay west to east and she now slept feet forward as the world turns. Before, she'd been spinning sideways through space.

In her newly positioned bed Louise sank into the murky world of sleep as if it were some actual place, a less substantial, but more powerful, realm. She came back reluctantly, as though emerging from anesthetic, trailing vivid metaphorical dreams that seemed to be parables or riddles posed by an oracle which she thought must contain truths or lessons if only she could decipher them. These she puzzled over like instruction manuals written in a foreign language.

She dreamt of baggage — suitcases and satchels and parcels, more than she could manage — of missing the bus and of a stranger inhabiting her basement and of crossing a desert in a white convertible. This image of the car possessed her. It was a sign, she thought, a spirit guide of the sort that appeared in the dream quests of Indian boys in the shape of a beckoning animal. Assigning guidance to another source, to mystical powers or a subconscious wish, relieved her of doubts that might otherwise have checked her, but even so she was afraid of spending too much money on the strength of a dream. She read the classifieds and drove long distances in the sensible Volvo to outlying areas where tattooed men with the sleeves ripped out of their shirts showed her beater Impalas with ragged tops, Skylarks, and once a Chrysler she almost bought, except the timing chain was bad. Long ago her first boyfriend, her high school boyfriend, had driven a salmon and white Imperial. She hadn't thought of him in years.

When sweepstakes offers arrived in the mail she followed the "not ordering" instructions, but sent her entry off in time to meet the early bird deadline. She applied for Bellagio, too, the Dobie-Paisano, Breadloaf, and other writers' retreats. She did these things as ends in themselves, not thinking about her chances once the envelope was mailed. The activity itself created the appearance of industry and optimism as if she believed in the future, as if she were planning for it, as if it mattered.

It was therefore a surprise when an invitation came from a film institute. At first she wasn't certain she would go. She wasn't sure she would benefit or that she had anything to contribute. It was difficult for her to talk about her work. And she didn't want to meet strangers. Before, when she'd gone out into the world in any way, she'd been married. Beloved of somebody. She'd had that like a veil between herself and the world. Now she felt peeled. There was nothing so exposed as an unmarried woman. She was certain she couldn't go.

Furthermore, the complications of leaving home overwhelmed her. She didn't know what to do with the boys, who would look after them, and who would feed the cat. Elliot would be in Greece on his honeymoon, unavailable.

Louise didn't feel as though she changed her mind about going, only that little solutions accreted to accommodate her absence until there was no very good reason not to go. Not going began to seem contrary and self-defeating.

You've *got* to go," Ingrid said. "Why ever wouldn't you? Maybe you'll meet someone."

"I don't want to meet anyone," Louise said. She was thinking of Richard, who had blazed through like a meteor. She wasn't yet ready to accept that he was gone or that the hole he'd punched in her life could be filled by anyone else.

"Well, forget meeting someone, then, just think of it as business, like something you *have* to do even if you don't want to. Like getting up and going to work." Ingrid was impatient with Louise's persistent dreamy gloom. She had volunteered to take the boys. She wanted Louise to dust herself off and get on with it. "It's only a week," she said. "It'll be good for you."

So before she knew it Louise had a departure date and a plane ticket and a ride to the airport. And she knew she was going. The obstacles she'd put in the way of it had been smoothed away.

She didn't want to let go of the boys. All good-byes had a desperate finality about them for Louise, as if she were a soldier or a pioneer and might never return, a trait she tried to hide because she knew it made her seem overly dramatic. Her father waved people out of sight flapping a handkerchief, a fluttering white flag if anyone looked back, visible longer than anything. She knew families who came and went without any ritual at all. This seemed very modern and possibly not very deep. But on this occasion her boys didn't mind at all that she was leaving — Ingrid was taking them to the shore — and she strove to be matter of fact.

It gave her an unlooked for lift to land in Salt Lake. Seattle had a lid on it, she realized, a low dome that weighed her down. She wondered if the gravitational pull of the earth was diminished at higher altitudes.

She was met and her bag was carried and she was driven up into the mountains. Summer camp for grownups, they called it. Normal concerns were left behind. Everybody was giddy. During the days they took themselves and each other seriously, meeting in various configurations to discuss their work with luminaries up from Los Angeles. In the evenings there were cocktails. Professional and romantic liaisons were rumored.

Louise had trouble engaging. Accustomed to solitude, working alone at home as she did, all the discussion and society rattled her. Even her work seemed abstract, as though it was somebody else's. In addition, she was preoccupied with the telephone and retreated to her cottage whenever she could. In some irrational way she believed that, having taken this little step out of herself and into the world, she would be rewarded by a longed for call from Richard. Perhaps her star would have risen and he might track her here. At the same time it seemed more likely that she'd return to a message than that the phone would actually ring in her presence. So beyond the meetings that were scheduled for her she required of herself that she go out and attend the social functions where she felt impossibly forlorn.

Outside on a deck built among the pines, she stood on the edge of things with a drink in her hand. Someone came around making introductions and left Louise with M., a foreign director, controversial for sex and violence, who was having a big success with his first American picture.

"What's it like to leave home?" she asked. "Speak a new language?" Feeling like a foreigner herself.

"Not so very difficult," he said. "One learns English at home, you know, in school. Everyone does."

"Will you go back?"

"Clearly," he said. "There's family still, and friends, of course. But not to live."

She thought it must be hard for his kids, who were the same ages as hers — this much she had learned already — and for his wife.

"No," he said, "apparently not. They like America."

They talked about school, as any parents would, and then she thought he'd drift off, but he didn't.

"It's more difficult for me, really," he said, taking the conversation back, "working with actors, trying to catch the nuance in a line. It's the inflection, you know, that you can't be certain of. Action pictures seem easier for the moment." He smiled. "A universal language."

"I know who you are, of course," she said after a silence, "but I haven't seen your work." She hadn't intended it the way she was afraid it sounded — insolent, challenging.

"There's a screening," he said. "You can come." Which was the other evening activity besides cocktails — looking at movies made by the visiting celebrities and quizzing them afterwards.

"I can't," Louise said, "I'm sorry."

"Why not?"

"I no longer can go to the movies," she told him. "I'm afraid I'll cry. I can't bear the sight of a kiss." She went on with the reasons, recounting things she'd never told anybody about Richard and Elliot and her divorce. She couldn't believe what she was saying. It was like an airplane conversation, your brain addled by drinks and boredom, a brief encounter when you revealed yourself to a stranger, someone you would never ordinarily meet. You left your life story in the lap of your astonished seat companion, as though, with a stranger, pride didn't enter into it. Normal reticence was abandoned. Louise was mortified. What he must think! He was looking at her oddly.

"In Europe it's more civilized," he said. "It's understood." Louise wasn't certain what he meant. Infidelity, she supposed. "Oh, well," she said, now wanting to flee, "It's all very boring unless you're me and then it's all you think about." And she laughed, trying to disown everything she'd disclosed. "Excuse me," she said. Walking away she thought, how awful; what had possessed her? But she shoved it out of her mind. Like Catholic sin erased by a Hail Mary, the embarrassment would vanish along with him. She'd never see him again.

Later she walked up the hill under the pines with Iris and Bruno, new friends who had taken her up like a goodwill project, and an Australian screenwriter and his wife. The air smelled of pitch and snow. Under normal circumstances it would be fun, she thought — the new friends, shared interests, career prospects. Now, though, there was no standard against which to sort experience. No one to talk to. She herself didn't provide a fixed point — she needed her husband for that, or Richard — somewhere to plant the compass foot. Whatever was happening took place relative to nothing, Zen-like, and then was lost.

In her cottage, during her absence, no one had called.

At the end of the week she went home and took up the quest for a car once more. One Saturday when her husband had the boys she rode the bus to Canada with ten one-hundred-dollar bills in her purse. At a vintage car auction in Langley she bid to her limit on every convertible that came on the block until the bidding stopped low on a beat-up Oldsmobile that was hers before she knew it. Other people had bought restored Mercurys and Auburns and hers was a rusted-out Cutlass. But the exchange rate was in her favor and the engine turned over and she completed the paperwork and put the top down. The engine noise resonated through holes in the muffler, reminding her again of old boyfriends, an earlier life.

In the current of air that washed over her as she drove homeward, she smelled turned fields and tide flats. She felt simultaneously connected and unfettered.

Idling in the line-up at the border, the Oldsmobile over-heated and stalled but a car full of teenagers behind her nudged it on through, and after it cooled for a while on the American side it started up again.

At home the neighbors came out and shook their heads but the boys thought she'd done a marvelous thing — signs of life, like fossils from Mars.

Five

WHEN THE BOYS were out of school Louise drove the
Oldsmobile to Los Angeles. "It won't make it," her mechanic
warned, "don't try it." And Jules, Ingrid's husband, supplied her
with flares, certain she'd break down. When she wanted a
cigarette one of the boys took the wheel, reaching across from
the passenger side while she ducked below the dash to strike a
match. The lighter didn't work, or the gas gauge, the idiot
lights, or speedometer. She surmised her speed by the flow of
traffic around her. But the radio blasted and they drove south
in July with the top down. Their noses peeled and blisters
ballooned on the tops of their ears. They stopped often to
check the oil and water — the vital fluids they called them —
and to top off the tank, swaggering into Quik Stops for iced tea
and Mountain Dew, grimy with sweat and dust like bikers or
travelers from another era.

In Los Angeles they stayed in Silverlake at the house of a
friend, Daphne, who was away. A blue house terraced into a
hillside three flights above the street. A Monterey cypress
beyond an arched window framed a view across downtown all
the way to the high-rise ghosts of Century City in the smog.
    Once there, Louise was preoccupied. She'd felt happy on
the way south, whizzing down the highway when all she had
to think about were practical and immediate concerns. But
now, here, she was disoriented, befuddled, as though she'd
taken a blow, reeling with a head full of asterisks like a cartoon
character. She went through the motions of life, attempting a
facade of normalcy for the sake of the boys. She shopped at an
unfamiliar market and cooked in a strange kitchen. The

smallest decision — what to have for dinner — stupefied her. Every meal she got on the table was a marvel. She woke early to work, writing while the boys still slept, sentences from somewhere crawling onto the screen. In the afternoons they went often to the beach where Louise watched with distracted tenderness as her children played in the surf, and sometimes she let them persuade her to swim as well, their enthusiasm overwhelming her lethargy. They eyed her furtively, alert for signs of despair. Security — her equilibrium — was paramount to them, subordinating other desires or complaints they might otherwise have voiced.

At night, after the boys were in bed, she sat outside in the dark on the patio smoking and sipping whiskey until she was numb enough to sleep. Out over the city helicopters hovered above the beams of their spotlights as though supported by pillars of light, each one a totem to some tragedy unfolding below.

Late one evening Louise left the boys asleep and the number by the phone and drove across Hollywood. Iris had called some days earlier, delighted she was in town. "Come to dinner, just a little dinner party. Meet some people." Louise had said yes but changed her mind and meant to call back and decline after all but forgot, let it slip, and now it was too late, she was expected, a place was set at the table. She would arrive late. She was driving fast, trying to make the lights.

Louise had lived in Los Angeles before with her husband, and the geography was imprinted in her memory like a circuit so that now she crossed the city by reflex. It was familiar too from more recent times when she'd been there on her own for meetings with agents or producers, or with Richard, another strata of memory with different landmarks and associations. Time was a strange dimension, inadequately comprehended, and it didn't seem impossible that a lifetime might fold back on itself, loop and coil like knitting. Driving west on Fountain she might pass her former self headed east, a different version of her weaving through the warp of years. She shook her head. She realized she was actually watching for the car, the old brown Volvo, and for her own head silhouetted beside Elliot's, coming home from the Troubadour or a movie in Westwood or dinner with the Sloyans, all those years before. If only she had paid attention or had had the right perspective, perhaps the future would have revealed itself then with as much clarity as she now remembered the past. Perhaps there'd been clues she'd missed along Fountain, or all over Los Angeles, as in pictures made for the entertainment of children containing startling hidden figures, fish swimming in treetops, ships navigating seas of tulips. The eye, the mind and imagination registered the expected and overlooked the rest.

Iris lived in West Hollywood. Her building was a piece of old California, a stucco complex of angles and archways built around a damp courtyard of buckled brick where elephant ears and bird-of-paradise leaned out, brushing Louise as she passed, and enormous carp circled sluggishly in a murky pond choked with water lilies.

Louise heard laughter and music from Iris's apartment upstairs and stood still for a moment in the dark courtyard, looking up at lighted French doors flung open onto a balcony. When she knocked and entered she'd laugh, too, and converse, and become for the moment whomever they thought her. It was a threshold to step across, from the comfort of her solitary interior world onto the stage of real life. She had to force herself to do it.

Vaulted ceilings, bare dark floor, soft white sofa, the guests around a heavy mission table. There was a moment of abeyance when Iris drew her in. Candlelit faces turned politely. Difficult to arrive late, require introductions, disrupt the dynamic in progress. A social occasion, a pleasure for some, obligation to others, to Louise a wave she could catch that would propel her through an evening, her volition suspended at the door. She slid into her place and conversation closed around her like water.

Swimming up from across the table came M.'s face. Amused eyes watching her. She had not expected to see him here or ever. She smiled and nodded as though he were not the repository of her life's story, and reached to shake his wife's hand.

Then later, a party in the backyard of a house in Santa Monica celebrating the birthday of Robert, the Australian screenwriter, collected like Louise into Iris's wide social net. Louise left the boys watching television while it was still light.

Summer in Los Angeles. Warm heavy air scented with jasmine and exhaust, girls in summer dresses, and overhead the rattle of palm fronds in the wind and the pervasive roar of traffic and planes, like the sea or blood in your ears. Passive as she was, cloistered by reserve, Louise might be an extra hired to populate the background of the scene the principals would play.

In the dusk on the patio M. approached her, his hands reaching to take her shoulders. Old acquaintances by now. He kissed her on each cheek. "How continental," she said. He laughed and kissed her lips.

"Shall we have lunch, then?" he asked, and then softly, lightly, though Bruno, standing close with her elbow still in his hand, or Iris, just beside him, might have heard, "Or would dinner be more romantic?"

To glimpse the future all you had was imagination. Imagination —Louise's — was so limited by distant and ingrained memory that it had become a part of personality and had ceased really to be imagination at all, molded as it was by disappointment and fear of disappointment. "Perhaps dinner," Louise murmured, surrendering to fate and to his initiative, nothing imagined and nothing yet to lose.

"When?"

She felt suddenly vague, beset. "I don't know," she said, "I'll call you. When the children go, perhaps."

Later she sat with him and his wife and others in the dark beside the pool, weirdly lit by wavering blue light cast by underwater lamps. An actress wound her arms and legs into a pretzel and tilted toward M., running her tongue along her teeth, her face close to his, an invitation to something. But beneath the table his knee touched Louise's and didn't shift away.

A stunt man who had arrived on crutches, dragging his legs like stove wood, struggled to his feet, wavered, then toppled backward into the pool — a body suddenly, unaccountably, spread-eagled in a brilliant turquoise rectangle, too garish for reality, so theatrical, so like a scene, that for moments no one moved. Then he gasped and flailed, churning water, paraplegic, and too drunk to help himself. It was Bruno, debonair in white ducks and an open shirt, who fished him out. Like a movie hero, never even wetting his cigarette. The actress clapped and transferred her attention to him.

Louise remained sitting in the dark, shaken, her knee grazing M.'s under the table. She never made a move. She wondered if she were capable.

At four in the morning Louise rose and drove the boys to LAX to fly home to Seattle and their father. She remembered her own annual pre-dawn drives from the Berkshires down the

Taconic Parkway to La Guardia, the ten-hour vibrating flight in a DC7 to San Francisco, and the obligatory disorienting six weeks each summer.

The traffic at that hour on the Santa Monica freeway surprised her. What was their business, all those people? Where were they going? She'd put the top up against the chill, the first time since leaving Seattle.

She'd routed the boys through Phoenix to save on the fare and she was back at Daphne's by the time they telephoned between planes. But her mind was already on the other call, the one she'd promised and had only waited to place until the boys were gone. Louise wondered what her mother had gotten up to in her own distant summers.

M.'s assistant said M. would have to call her back. She hung up. The anathema of waiting. Desire burgeoned with the possibility of disappointment. She was already missing the boys. Their departure, moments before a liberation, now became instantly a privation. But the phone rang almost immediately. He sounded businesslike and distracted, but they settled on an evening and a restaurant.

Louise went beforehand to a gallery opening where she looked at paintings over the rim of a champagne glass. She was alone among the collectors — the glitter of diamonds in everybody's ears, the drape of Armani, and the scent of Chloé piercing her with a memory of her mother. She was severed, a long way distant from anything familiar, the house in Silverlake remote as though it were on another planet, the boys and her own house in Seattle at an impossible remove, no longer anything to do with her.

When she'd dressed at Daphne's the sun was still shining outside and she was warm and indolent from the bath. In the car the vinyl seat held the warmth of the sun and cupped her like a palm, the wind was warmer than flesh against her skin. Now she wished she hadn't said she'd come, or that it was already over with, behind her. It was like the dentist or any other kind of ordeal, something to be gotten through. It would be awkward, there'd be nothing to say, he'd be bored, or she would be. It seemed now that she'd misunderstood or given the wrong impression.

Louise left the gallery. Beverly Hills was vacated, the streets empty, the shoppers departed, and the diners yet to come. The click of her heels accompanied her to her car.

She found the restaurant and let the attendant park the car, a legacy from Richard, though she could have found space on the street. She had arrived before him. It was early, the restaurant empty, an inelegant hour for dinner. He was wedging her in at the end of the day, a late appointment that could be explained at home, not romantic at all. She waited at the bar, alone with the staff and their carefully vacant stares, a cast of thousands and only her to serve. She studied her reflection through a curl of smoke. She wished she'd worn a hat and a dark slash of lipstick, a wall of aplomb. Or pants. She was fragile in her dress. Perhaps he wouldn't come. She wouldn't give him long.

He was shorter than she remembered when he arrived, breezing in, standing at her shoulder, not touching, more handsome in a rumpled way, more professorial than glamorous. He smiled but didn't hold her eyes.

"Hi."

"Hi."

"You found it all right?"

"As you can see."

She sounded cool on purpose but he laughed. And then allowed them to be led immediately to a table, her wine glass following on a tray. In a hurry, she thought, as she was, eager to have it over.

Like a good soldier shouldering up the burden of conversation, she inquired about his children, his projects, movies he'd seen and liked, what he'd read, just as you'd inquire of anyone for politeness' sake to fill the march of time until escape. No tolerance for silence, she hated that about herself. All the conventional information, but he talked about the war too, his childhood — bombs and shortages — the move to the States, difficulties. The restaurant filled up around them and was empty again when they left. She'd lost track of time. Too much wine and a sambuca on the house.

"Shall we walk a little?" he asked outside, and took her arm. Difficult to walk for the first time with a new companion. The solution, as in dancing, malleability, a compliance to his lead. Louise unbent like warmed plastic against his side. He stopped and turned her to him, kissed her. She closed her eyes and thought about their lips, his tongue, his teeth bumping hers, the fit of their mouths together, the exploratory nature of a kiss, another sort of conversation, so much information exchanged.

Across the street in a park they leaned against a wall like lovers, arms at their sides and fingers intertwined as they kissed, on and on. Then later, lying on the grass, her dress up around her waist, the pale moon of her hip glowing like a melon on the lawn. Footsteps. Someone walking past. They waited, looking into each other's eyes, barely breathing, listening. Alone again, they laughed against each other. He smoothed her skirt back into place and pulled her to her feet.

The parking valet had despaired of her return, abandoned her car in front of the restaurant, the keys beneath the mat. It was three in the morning. Louise wondered what M. would tell his wife.

She drove home across town with the top down, the warm night wrapped around her like a stole. The next day she woke appalled, her head raging, lips bruised and her cheeks chapped — whisker burn they'd called it as kids — afraid he'd call and afraid he wouldn't.

Silverlake was an area of modest bungalows tiered into the hills north of downtown, emerging from a shabby past into gentrification. The streets wound up the old drainages and climbed like runners up among the stacked houses.

Daphne had returned. She and Louise read the paper and drank their coffee in hazy morning sunshine on the patio beside the blue house. City noises — the muted roar of the Hollywood freeway, a distant siren, a car alarm futilely persisting, and then closer, the whining grind of an approaching garbage truck. They looked up from the paper. Thursday. They'd forgotten. They jumped up and hurried. There was still time, the truck had not yet reached them. They ran barefoot down the flights of stairs in their nightgowns, the week's newspapers and the kitchen trash bundled in their arms. The men on the truck grinned when they saw them and shouted something Louise couldn't hear, amiable black men amused by their haste and dishabille. She waved and smiled.

They returned to their coffee and the newspaper, out of breath and flushed by the exertion. A tiny unease pricked at the back of Louise's mind, as of something forgotten or neglected. She ignored it. She was happy.

Le Dôme, earlier in the week. A place to be seen at lunch. All eyes flicked to her as she wound among the tables, lost interest, then registered her again when she slid in opposite

M., her stock rising by association. Here no one forgot a face. She'd lodge in a dozen brains for future reference like a card in Concentration.

She was embarrassed, hot, toying with her fork, imagining that he superimposed lunch to eradicate dinner and its aftermath, which was the reason she had said she'd come, hoping to regain possession of herself. She glanced at him from under her eyes. He was smiling. "So," he said, "shall we have an affair, then?"

It wasn't what she had expected . . . although she didn't know what she *had* expected. She laughed. Business negotiations like at all the other tables. She thought about it, or pretended to. Actually, from the moment he spoke, she knew what she would do, but she turned it over, the worldliness of it. She felt like a girl essaying sophistication in her mother's pumps, afraid she'd trip, give herself away. He was watching her. "Sure," she said then, handing herself over — not to him, but to the experiment — delivering herself up to adventure.

"What about the risks?" he asked. Like truth in advertising, she thought, full disclosure. Sign a release form before the bungie jump.

"What risks? There isn't any risk for me," Louise said. "I'm single. I can do as I wish. No one cares."

"Not practical risks," he said. "But you might want more. You know, become attached."

"Oh, that," she said, waving her hand, dismissing the possibility. But she thought about the implication. "That's not a risk for you?"

"No," he said, "it isn't." He touched her hand. "We could be friends, if you prefer."

"Like what?" she asked. "Have lunch occasionally? Chat?"

He nodded, looking at her. "Clearly." As in any negotiations, indifference determined advantage and she was certain he could walk away and only mind a little.

She had, beginning Thursday, for three weeks, a borrowed apartment on the edge of Beverly Hills, off Doheny below Santa Monica. One of her agents was going to France. A place of her own, a venue. She wrote the address out for him on the coaster. "We must be very careful," M. said. But after lunch he kissed her for a long time out on Sunset in front of Le Dôme where anyone might have seen.

It seemed to Louise that Los Angeles was part of the collective unconscious, universal, like dreams of bears and flight, so there was the constant shock of recognition. Brad's apartment was like that, instantly familiar as though she'd lived there before. Set back from the street on the ground level, it had a generic comfort. She had been given keys and instructions for lights, timers, watering, mail, laundry, emergencies — a careful list on a yellow tablet for all eventualities which Brad would leave for her on the kitchen counter.

Now Thursday had arrived. In a little while she would collect her things, load the car, thank Daphne, and drive across town. M. would come at three.

Louise couldn't find her hairbrush. She thought she knew what she'd done: she carried it with her in the convertible and the day before she'd come home with flowers and wine and sacks of groceries for a farewell dinner with Daphne, and exquisite new underpants for herself in a department store bag. Too many parcels, too much to carry, her hands full. She'd rested it all on the fender, consolidating the load, not wanting to make more than one trip up the stairs. She had dropped the brush in with the groceries, sliding it down between the plastic and the paper. Now she checked in the kitchen but as she thought, they'd used the bag for trash. It was a small matter. She had another brush.

Then later, after a shower, she dressed and was ready to go. Her things were by the door — briefcase and valise, garment bag and computer. Daphne would help her carry it all down.

She must return Daphne's house key. And that was the moment when she knew, standing by the door, even before she looked, that she wouldn't find her keys. She knew what she'd done. It was the reason for the earlier worm of anxiety. To free her hands she had dropped the keys into the grocery bag along with the hair brush, the bag was used for trash, so she was complicit when she hurried to catch the garbage truck at the curb. Her vigilant subconscious, thwarting her plans, making manifest her ambivalence, had caused her to throw away her car keys, Seattle house keys, Daphne's key, and alas, Brad's apartment keys. Deliberately, irrevocably toss them out with the trash. Her first impulse was to laugh and salute her subconscious as though she were a divided person and there was a jealous and triumphant sister inside her.

But she didn't *feel* ambivalent. And not yet ready to concede. She poured tequila and orange juice and tried to think. When she left Seattle, in an afterthought, she'd run back into the house for the spare ignition key and had zipped it into her purse. She looked and it was there; she could still drive. But Brad's apartment? If she called M. and told him, wouldn't he have thought better of it anyway? He wouldn't suggest a hotel or a postponement, he'd say it was off, over before it began, better this way.

Daphne left for work. She didn't understand the tragedy. She wouldn't have had patience for it anyway, handling her own divorce differently, finished with men, learning to ride and to play polo. "Stay another night," she said, "or as long as you want. No big deal."

Louise called her agency, where Brad was an associate. He was on his way to France, airborne, and had left no spare keys.

Louise couldn't remember the name of the landlady, though she could picture it written on the tablet left lying on the counter, along with a telephone number in case of emergency, somewhere distant, outlying. Eaglerock or Torrance. The building had no resident manager.

Louise sat down with the yellow pages. It was eleven in the morning. He was coming at three. She could feel the tequila. There were a million locksmiths in Los Angeles, all advertising twenty-four-hour service, lock-out service for all the screw-ups, all the locks and deadbolts devised for security that shut people out, a whole industry erected on the pediment of ineptitude. But it wasn't her apartment, and she had no identification connecting her to that address. No one wanted to take a chance on her story.

Finally — it took persuasion, pleading, and a corroborating call to the agency — West Hollywood Locksmiths was having a slow day and agreed to dispatch a lock picker to Brad's address where she was to meet him. She flew across town.

"Stan" was embroidered on his coverall. He was beefy and suspicious, watching Louise with skeptical eyes, studying her for signs of malfeasance while his thick fingers manipulated tiny picks inserted in the lock. Sometimes, he told her, locks were installed upside down and couldn't be picked. Louise watched him in silence for long moments, anxiety building, then she heard the tumbler fall. She was in! "Hallelujah," Stan said dryly. She hugged him and he grinned.

She had time enough for another shower, time to collect her wits and simulate nonchalance. At three-thirty she thought he wasn't coming. Then he walked in without knocking and took her in his arms and kissed her.

How odd to sleep with a stranger in a strange apartment in the middle of the afternoon. It was like an erotic dream, a fantasy or like a matinee or a headache, an episode unrelated to the rest of life, unintegrated with normal experience. At once intense and impersonal.

M. held her by her wrists, her arms stretched wide as she rocked beneath him, and his look, his eyes locked on hers, not rolled inward but searching hers for ardor, for reciprocal arousal, was a more intimate connection than his penis inside her. It shocked her, won her. Not looking at her body, her breasts, her mouth or below where they were joined, but into her eyes where she couldn't hide. His look insisted upon complicity, made her his confederate and bound her to him.

The following weeks elapsed like an intermezzo between the acts of her real life. The light was golden, the air heavy and soft against her skin. It was warm and quiet when she went out in the mornings to move her car in compliance with Beverly Hills parking restrictions. During the night oleanders dropped pink blossoms into the convertible and spangled the hood like a ceremonial car. She never met the neighbors but her awareness of their activities and routines was palliative, their normalcy mitigating her solitude. She worked in the mornings at her computer until slatted sunlight falling through the Venetian blinds obscured the screen. M. came in the afternoons and left while it was still light. She walked out with him, barefoot in her jeans, and kissed him in the twilight beneath the sycamores. She didn't like to let him go, dreaded the moment when he pulled away and she watched him out of sight, then turned to go in and found his absence salient in the empty apartment.

She didn't tell M., didn't want him to know, though she didn't know why, but sometimes in the evening she walked up the hill to Sunset and rented a video of one of his movies, and took it home, climbing back into Brad's rumpled sheets to watch. Her own private retrospective. She rented her own movie once too, but didn't get past her own name — *written by* — in the credits. It made her think of Richard and of a time when she was still married and might yet have chosen differently.

"I think he likes you," Iris said out of the blue. They were eating lunch at Hugo's.

"Who?"

An exasperated look from Iris. "What did he say to you at Robert and Liz's?"

"What do you mean? We didn't really talk."

"I thought you were going to have dinner or something."

"Lunch. We did." Learning to lie.

"And?"

"And nothing. Just lunch. Chit chat. He's nice."

"You know he has a reputation," Iris said.

"A reputation for what?"

"For screwing around."

Louise lit a cigarette. The matches were from Le Dôme. "I didn't know. He's married anyway."

"Even so," said Iris. Then after a moment, "I never see you. I thought I'd see more of you."

"I know, me too. But I've been working, you know. Deadlines."

"Bruno has a friend —"

"No," said Louise, "Please. I'm not ready for that."

And then her time was up. What had seemed like a wealth of days, a thick sheaf, had thinned down and was gone. In the morning she scrubbed the tub, washed the sheets and towels, and remade the bed for Brad. She vacuumed, erasing her presence, leaving nothing of herself but a footprint in the carpet's pile on her way to the door. Outside she stood for a long time on the stoop, the keys she'd had cut in her hand, waiting for the moment when she could make herself let go, drop them through the mail slot and close the door on a chapter.

She parked at a meter on Sunset and dodged across the street to a Japanese restaurant where she was meeting M.. Lunch, a propriety to balance turpitude. Inside it was all clean planes and angles and clinical light. You were on display here, a bug in a jar. You could do surgery. There was nothing on the plate Louise recognized and her chopsticks betrayed her. She sipped tea from a thimble. She should have had a belt of something before she came.

He held her hand when they left and led her up along the winding residential streets above the restaurant, above the Strip. She liked it about him that he liked to walk. It made him seem more ordinary. They sat down on a curb and kissed in the sunlight. It was flat and bright, like pop art — a Hockney painting — like the beginning of a migraine and nothing to take the edge off. Their feet were in the gutter. She wanted a cigarette. It should be dawn or stormy, tattered clouds racing in a violet sky, something to match her Wagnerian interior. Clinging to each other before they were sundered. Instead, she wanted to escape, to be alone in the car, but she couldn't make herself let go, be the one. When she left, that would be it. Over. Finito. Or so she thought.

"So," he said, smiling.

"So?"

"Time to go?"

"Yes. I guess."

He stood and pulled her to her feet.

Back on Sunset he was in a hurry to be off, back to the office and whatever his afternoon held. "Bye, then," he said with his little lilt. She didn't wait for his car to come, but cut back through the traffic to where she'd left the Olds. There was a parking ticket on the windshield. A raspberry from the municipality. Valet parking would have been a bargain. M. tooted the horn and blew her a kiss across four lanes of traffic as he pulled away.

She drove into Hollywood then and cut up into the hills, back in time. She had chosen a color for the house called Jersey Cream and planted sycamores, one for each baby, out in front. Decisions of great moment at the time. The trees had grown up and were throwing mottled shade and now the bungalow was gray. She wondered if it was true that every seven years each cell in the body was replaced. She was a different person now, nearly twice over. Even the memory seemed second hand.

She found her way over the hill into the Beachwood canyon, making turns from memory, like an old horse, without having to think. Up past the market, more tiny streets, a hairpin the Oldsmobile couldn't manage where she lodged crosswise and had to back up and maneuver. It was quaint and perilous, like trying to drive in Italy, streets made for donkeys or Fiats.

Richard lived in a stucco house plastered into the contour of the hill like a cliff dwelling, its back to the street like the wall of a fortress. She stopped and got out. There was a hibiscus planted in a terra cotta jar by the door. Inside the scarlet trumpets the stamens strained upward with the scimitar curve of an erection. Louise stared.

They had said good-bye — one of their good-byes — with a toast of champagne, standing on his balcony as the sun went down. He had drained his glass and flung it far out so it cleared the patio below and landed unheard somewhere down the hill.

He lived his life as though people were watching, made a ceremony of everything. But Louise thought he'd look for the glass the next day, hoping to find it unharmed in the arms of the chaparral. Still, he had shattered her.

She wondered what she was doing. It was like trying to see if she was alive, pin pricks to assess nerve damage. Can you feel this? This? Dead, right up to the present moment.

Above the reservoir, on the back way over the hills, she stopped and stepped out of her skirt and pulled on her jeans, climbing back into her own skin, getting comfortable. She thought of her mother unhooking her bra and pulling it out of the neck of her dress the instant she walked into the house. Eucalyptus on the hot air smelled like spirits that would ignite if you struck a match.

Louise was on the Hollywood freeway and headed north by three, ahead of the rush, out through Sylmar where freeway ramps ended in midair like installation art, something dreamed up by Christo, a metaphor for the perils and pointlessness of the city. She crossed the mountains and dropped down the Grapevine into the San Joaquin Valley where long ago her husband had invested in land against her wishes and made his one and only killing.

Somewhere north on I-5 the Oldsmobile overheated; the fluid churning in the radiator was choked with silt, percolating thickly. At a Texaco in Gilroy, the garlic capitol a sign announced, they were too busy to help her but a Mexican boy, one of the mechanics, gave her a hose and told her what to do. Out behind the station, the hood up and the engine running, the hose stuck down in the radiator to flush the system, a hot wind spattering muddy coolant across her sandals, dust in her eyelashes and grit between her teeth, a light bulb suddenly came on. She'd been thinking it was over but it didn't have to be. If she wanted she could call M. She could call now from the pay phone outside the service bay or a month from now. She could say she was coming back. He wouldn't say no. He'd be glad. She looked around with new eyes, felt the wind like a hand up under her shirt.

When the water ran clear the boy came out and lay down on his back and hitched himself under the car to thread the drain plug back in place. When he stood up his shirt was wet and she brushed off his back, and felt the sharp ridges of his shoulder blades beneath her palm. He smiled and murmured, "Gracias, Señora." A crescent of white showed below the iris of his eyes, implying melancholy, Louise thought.

She bought fresh coolant and poured it in. Then she scrubbed her hands in the washroom. When she came out she stood beside the telephone. She'd memorized M.'s office number. But the Mexican boy and the smell of gas and grease and exhaust had reminded her of other things. She rifled the pages of the thin directory, looking for her first boyfriend's name, though why he'd be in Gilroy, California she had no idea. There was nothing listed that was even close.

Further on, after she'd passed through Sacramento and it had gotten dark, the engine froze up as she drove. The power steering and brakes went out and she hauled on the wheel and coasted to the shoulder. She lifted the hood and smelled hot metal. She lit a flare and held it aloft for light but couldn't determine the problem.

She got a tow into Willows and called the boys. She didn't know what was wrong and had no idea how long she'd be delayed. Her younger son started to cry as soon as he heard her voice. He'd fallen off the porch and broken his wrist and had spent the afternoon in the emergency room. Louise didn't wait for morning. For once in her life she made a quick decision. She signed the pink slip over to the towing company and sat up in the bus terminal until the wee hours when a northbound Greyhound rolled through.

Six

SUMMER WAS NEARLY gone, just the last tail of August remained, in the northern latitudes the most piquant time of year. Louise took the boys to the family's summer house on an island in the Sound. The sand was still hot in the afternoons but the light fell at a slant and leathery madrone leaves rattled down in every breeze. The flyway was busy with migratory flocks traveling south, arriving and departing. The island was an ornithological Grand Central. Sanderlings patrolled the shore, precise as drill teams. Out on the water loons called. The orchard smelled of cider and hummed with drunken wasps. It was dangerous to walk there. At night phosphorescence lit the tide line and illuminated the wake of a swimmer or a canoe paddle. The water was very cold but they swam in the afternoon when the tide had come up over the heated sand and sometimes at night when the moon rose out of the crater of Mount Rainier.

Louise's brother was there with his family, her sister with hers, and her father and stepmother and friends in cottages up and down the beach. They wandered in and out of each other's kitchens and settled on each other's porches, resuming conversations begun the previous year. They drank martinis and jug wine and were tipsy all the time.

Louise slid a plastic veterinary glove manufactured for pregnancy testing of cattle over her son's arm and taped it above the elbow to keep sand out of his cast. She took a book and a bottle of wine to the beach.

Here, more than in San Francisco, Louise felt part of something. Her boys were happy. There were friends and cousins for them to play with and other adults besides her who rounded out the world. They sailed and fished and engineered dikes against the tide. The absence of their father went unnoticed. Louise too, was happy. Happy-ish, as she put it to herself. But she was divided, not completely there. At night they took turns scanning the skies through her brother's telescope. They saw meteor showers in the Pleiades and the moons of Jupiter. That was her, she thought, a long way distant, circling aimlessly.

There was no telephone, but sometimes late at night when the boys were asleep Louise drove the narrow winding roads off the island to call her answering machine from the Spencer's Lake tavern. One time there was a message, M.'s voice: "Have a nice holiday, bye-bye, and a kiss."

In celebration, she let a logger buy her a glass of Schlitz before she headed back. She had crossed the bridge and was back on the island when a deer leapt into her path. She was driving too fast. She braked but there wasn't enough time. The deer came up over the Volvo's hood and slid sideways across the windshield, blinding her, and somersaulted off the driver's side. Louise got the car stopped. A headlight was out and the remaining one shot a cone of light off into the woods. Her heart was hammering.

Years before in Wyoming she'd gone poaching with her boyfriend, trying for an out-of-season deer. You could get one right along the highway, get it frozen in your lights long enough to squeeze off a shot, bleed it and gut it in the dark, cram it into the trunk and head back to town. The sheriff was onto him, keeping an eye out, so they used her car. Her boyfriend needed the deer. There was a whole family of younger brothers and sisters to feed.

That deer was dead by the time they came up to it. But now she didn't know. She was afraid to get out of the car. Afraid of what she'd find. She imagined terrible wounds, thrashing legs. She wouldn't know what to do. She had neither gun nor flashlight. She urgently wanted the deer to be dead. She felt incapable of dealing with an injured deer, of bludgeoning it on into oblivion with the tire iron. Playing God. She didn't feel like God, she felt like God's instrument, as though responsibility for the deer was the price He exacted in return for M.'s message. One hand gave and the other took away.

She got out and stood by the door while her eyes adjusted, then walked a little distance down the road in the direction she'd come. She wasn't even certain of the spot, how far she might have traveled after the impact. She stood in the dark listening, wondering what to do. The road wound away in a dark ribbon between the darker trees bordered by a pale fringe which was Queen Anne's lace growing along the berm.

In the end she drove away. There was nothing to see, nothing to do. The next day she drove back out past where she thought it had happened, turned the car around, and crept slowly back, but even then she couldn't visualize the spot. Everything was different in daylight. She stopped the car and waded through the weeds on the shoulder of the road. She listened for flies and looked for blood on the pavement. Somewhere in the woods the deer was dead or dying or suffering or mending. She wouldn't ever know. Now a criminal feeling contaminated her thoughts of M. When she remembered his voice on her message machine the thud of impact came back to her as well. If things were different, if she were married, if she hadn't somehow relinquished her legitimacy, she'd tell about the deer and she'd be an object of sympathy.

Back at the cottage, she parked head-in against a huckleberry thicket to hide the damage, but eventually someone asked about the headlight and she spun a lie that incorporated a daylight trip to Spencer's Lake and the gas pumps there, a pickup and someone else's stupidity, a story so detailed and convoluted that no one doubted its veracity.

During most of the year Louise had the use of the cottage —
none of the rest of them lived close enough — but for the
period in the summer when the family congregated there she
slept dormitory-style with her boys on a row of mattresses in
the barn loft above the old boats and broken lawn furniture, the
lawn mower, chain saw, and rubbish containers. It smelled of
gas and garbage and damp, unused except for the few weeks
each summer when her sister displaced her. At night Louise
could hear the boys breathing and turning in their sleep, mice,
and, more distantly, coyotes yodeling at the bottom of the
orchard where they came to eat the blackberries. In the
morning there was blue scat on the path.

On the Saturday of the Labor Day weekend they went to
the Grange Hall dance, packed into Louise's brown Volvo,
squeezed together with kids on laps as though no one knew
any better. Louise knew the lyrics to "Lucille" by heart — an
esoteric feat in the eyes of her more urbane relations — and
she belted through them twice on the way with help on the
chorus the second time through from her passengers. "Four
hungry children and a crop in the field/you picked a fine time
to leave me, Lucille."

There was now always a slight unpleasant frisson on the
stretch of road where she'd hit the deer. She slowed down.

Later her brother-in-law gave the band five dollars to play
something, *anything*, in three-quarter time and when he
couldn't find his wife he took Louise for a spin around the
floor. He'd been drinking beer out of the trunk of the car all
night and he lay his cheek against hers holding her closer than
she liked as they waltzed. She wondered if it was her sister's
carryings-on that gave him license, or her own divorce. He
might subtly prey on her perceived vulnerability or hope to

pique her sister. Either way she didn't like it. Her taboos were lined up like soldiers in formation no matter what anyone else did. She liked her brother-in-law, but didn't want him locking his hipbone into hers when they twirled. She knew he'd regret it in the morning.

The summer people attended the Grange Hall dance like gentry observing a quaint folk ritual. Like the sand dollar collections and agates and moon snail shells, an account of it could be trotted out in Boston or San Francisco as evidence of a fabulous vacation. Louise, however, was torn, her loyalties compromised. She had a foot in both worlds.

When she lived in Wyoming, which was a chapter of her life no one in her family comprehended, on Saturday nights in the summers she went to the Woods Landing dances where sawyers came in from the logging camps and mingled with cowboys and college boys working for the Forest Service. Wild, underage kids like her drove thirty miles out from town because they knew they'd be served in the bar. Sometimes boys rolled their cars on the way home. Louise's boyfriend had a scar along his eyebrow where he'd gone through the windshield, and a white cross on the side of the highway marked the spot where a Candeleria boy hadn't walked away.

At Woods Landing Louise learned the schottische in the arms of an inarticulate Finn and slow danced with her boyfriend, not moving, just shifting from foot to foot, their arms locked around each other. When the band played a fast one the town boys backed up against the walls or went out to the parking lot to drink or fight between the cars and the girls took over the floor and jitterbugged wildly with the cowboys or with each other.

Once at Woods Landing Louise encountered Lloyd McCullough, her driver's ed teacher, also the basketball coach and assistant principal of her high school and the father of a girl in her class. He'd been fishing and drinking beer all day. He showed her the trout packed in ice in a cooler in the trunk, which was weird enough, and then asked her to get into the car with him and she did, even though she knew she shouldn't. He smelled of bay rum and looked like Robert Mitchum and at school she called him Sir. She'd never seen him before when he wasn't wearing a suit. He'd had her in to the principal's office before for cutting class. Now he put his hand against her face and she smelled fish and she thought she might faint. "One kiss," he said, and when she tried to pull away he reached past her shoulder and locked the door. He was bigger than the boys she knew and his weight engulfed her. She couldn't catch her breath. She struggled against him, but she'd never had so much attention paid to her by a grown man and the thrill made her limp. She gave up and let him kiss her, mostly because she wanted him to, but partly because she was amazed he'd risk it and she wanted to know how far he'd take it. Afterwards he lifted his arm off her shoulder, lay it along the top of the seat, and tipped his head back and closed his eyes. He didn't try to stop her when she slid away and slipped out of the car.

After that at school sometimes she saw him watching her as she passed his office between classes. It was the first she knew of how she might draw a man, a bruised seeming girl who could keep a secret. She stopped caring that Rita, his daughter, and her clique of friends didn't include her. She felt a hundred years older than they, and she walked through the halls with her chin in the air, cutting class with impunity.

Through the fall and winter Louise found it easy to skip to Los Angeles for a day or two here and there. Elliot wanted more time with the boys, or said he did, and demanded every third

51

week with them. Louise thought he wanted to avoid child support, which she believed, as all divorced mothers did, he confused with alimony and withheld for fear of benefiting her. Men's hearts were turnips, in her estimation. And so, though she didn't wish for it, she thus had blocks of time when she wasn't needed at home.

In L.A. she stayed with Iris or Daphne or with Moira, another friend, but always with an interlude at a hotel with M. Sometimes there was some legitimate business that took her south, but often there was no purpose other than him.

In this way she lost days out of her life, gaps when no one knew where she was. If anyone had checked she'd have left the screen like an aircraft in the Bermuda triangle. Her boys thought she was at Moira's, Moira thought she was in Seattle, but in fact, she was checked into a hotel in West Hollywood where no one would ever think to look. She could vanish and never be traced.

She asked for a room on the street side — such an odd request it could usually be accommodated. White noise, she explained, the sound of traffic soothing as waves, like a room at the shore; and that preference went into the dossier they kept in the computer along with Moira's number, which she gave as her own, and the method of payment, which was cash.

She smoked on the balcony while she waited for M., watching for him to appear at the top of the street, afraid he wouldn't come. He walked over from his office and her heart surged each time when he hove into sight. An ordinary pedestrian was what he appeared to be, an interesting, intelligent-looking man lost in thought as he proceeded on his way. Passers-by were never the same to her after, concealing as they might the nature of their errands. She wished he'd look up and see her and smile, but he never did. Watching him without his knowledge was like photographing an Indian, she thought: it diminished him and inculpated her, captured something of him she wasn't entitled to.

They spent long experimental erotic afternoons together which, to Louise, seemed paradoxically innocent. Like animals or children. Afterwards they slept. Or he slept. She lay still beside him. He dreamed and she wondered of what, his eyes racing around under his lids. She wished she could sleep and wished she were more easily satisfied. The playful intimacy of sex together wasn't enough, she wanted to possess him or become him, secure him somehow. She kept this to herself, however, and played by his rules and never mentioned love. If he knew how she felt he'd no longer trust her not to eat him.

When she rolled out from under his leg he stirred and reached for her. "Tell me about your life," he said, his eyes closed, like asking for a story.

"There's nothing to tell."

"Tell me about your writing."

"It goes along."

"Put in more sex, you'll have more success."

When she didn't answer he opened his eyes to see if she was smiling. She was. "Thank you for the advice," she said.

"What about a boyfriend?"

"No."

"Why not?"

"What do I want with a boyfriend?" she asked. "Anyway, I'm not interested. I have you."

This was a joke and he smiled, as she'd meant him to, but he squeezed her and said, "It's not enough."

"For me it is, for the moment."

Then he'd take her to dinner at one of the famous restaurants, which both flattered and offended her. Once he laughed out loud and wouldn't tell her why, then later in the car when she pressed him he said that he had noticed that everyone else in Mr. Chow's was a middle-aged man with a mistress. After that Louise wouldn't go out anymore except to walk up the street to the Mirabelle where they didn't need a reservation and she could wear jeans and they could sit outside.

He told her about his work and gave her the script for his new picture, sketching story board sequences in the margins while he talked. When she read it she didn't find the existential themes he claimed ran through the plot, but she loved the moon-faced men he drew in pencil armed with Uzis, the terrain of Mars and his three-breasted women. Her own Picasso, she thought, idly doodling a treasury for her.

She mined him for information, learning as much as she could, interrogating him easily, conversationally extracting pieces of past and present to fit together into the picture of a life as though she might inhabit him. In this way she was easy to be with, inquiring politely, listening attentively, a pleasant companion. There was nothing in particular she sought. She didn't weight information in terms of importance; it was volume, mass. She fed on him — an undetected parasite, with the voracity of a carnivorous plant.

But when he asked she deflected questions about herself, retreating as though leaving a room. She was contained, fluid in a bottle that might spill and never be recovered. Confessions or confidences would deplete her, and once started, like a siphon, she wouldn't stop until she was sucked dry and there was nothing left of her. What felt dense and heavy like mercury, centering her like a child's inflated clown that couldn't be upset, might shatter, dissipate, or vaporize, seem trivial, and lose its ability to right her. She moved within a field, grounded by a core of heavy metal.

It felt genteel to keep possession of so much of herself. She felt grown up, entirely separate and completely safe. She imagined herself in black, in a hat, a woman with a secret or a past, deliberate, calm, reflected in polished brass as she checked in at the hotel desk, the sound of her heels in the hallway, the measured rhythm of a long unhurried stride. In her valise a grenade, a manuscript, a pint of gin. In the room white curtains billowed at the window, the afternoon heat held a charge like electricity, a promise of explosion. The heavy suspense of waiting, the collision when he came.

In his absence, before he arrived or when she was at home in Seattle or anywhere, times with him seemed like dreams recalled or episodes of hallucination, as though sometimes an exotic stranger took possession of her, used her person for adventure and then departed, leaving behind a little residue of memory to tantalize her like déjà vu, imperfect recollections of a different and more desirable incarnation. She hoarded match books, hotel lotions, and shampoos as tangible evidence, bits of the spacecraft, and used them sparingly to call back images and reinforce memory. She preserved his voice on her answering machine tapes.

Seven

IN THE FRACTION of a second after Louise asked, "How shall I recognize him?" she spun an entire mental fiction. He'd wear a rose or carry a placard. Or she would. She saw herself in a hat. An ordinary encounter blossomed with romance as she imagined the mechanics of identification. She leapt into the future a stranger's wife.

Her father had anticipated exactly this question and now delivered a preformed reply like an egg. "Giles Swan is short," he said, "and he will be immediately recognizable because, through blindness or vanity, his toupee is many shades darker than his own fringe of hair." It was the way he spoke, in sentences and paragraphs composed on a mental page and read back slowly, not hesitatingly, just deliberately. If you broke in to supply a word to hurry him along, anticipating the end of his thought, he'd subside into silence, sensitive as a snail's horn.

"Oh," Louise said, and adjusted the stranger in her imagination. There'd be no need for the rose. "How did you describe me?" she asked.

"Tall, blond, and pretty," he replied, and she was surprised he had any image of her ready at hand. She'd have guessed he'd have to ponder in order to bring her up on his screen, or that he'd offer character traits — aggrieved, resentful.

When they hung up she tried to fit herself into her father's description, but it was her sister who came to mind. Her younger half-sister in the hat, bristling with pheasant feathers and assurance. Louise didn't carry around a vision of herself, of her exterior, what she presented to the world. Her self, to herself, was wholly internal.

In the Midland airport Louise and Mr. Swan approached each other without hesitation. Louise slid her eyes away, afraid she'd laugh. She hadn't really believed in the toupee — she'd thought her father exaggerated or had made it up — but it curled around Mr. Swan's head like an animal, a sleeping ferret, more startling than anything she could have pictured, more hat than wig. A toque like a matador's. She couldn't have missed him. She wondered who he had for friends that let him go around like this.

She stood back and kept her distance, out of kindness she supposed, to allow a more level gaze. Mr. Swan was indeed extremely short.

He took possession of her bag and led her out.

The car was at the curb, the reason she was there, more car than she had pictured. A dun-colored Lincoln chosen to silently eat up the Texas miles and never show the dust.

An inventory had come in the mail enumerating possessions left to Louise's father by his brother-in-law, her uncle Marion. A mahogany breakfront, a ball-and-talon-footed dining room set, an upright piano, a Lalique vase, a bedroom suite, cadillac desk, console TV, computer, and on and on. Marion's Towncar was on the list and a Crown Victoria from the fifties.

Louise's father wanted none of it except the vase, but he composed the list and sent copies to his children, asking each of them what they wanted. Dealing with this list seemed complicated and challenging to Louise. Suppose they all wanted the same thing? And although she realized it was impractical and perhaps false, still it seemed unmannerly to desire things, objects, made available by a death. Unless, of course, you could attribute the wish for something of Marion's to sentiment, which none of them could, since they'd hardly known him. Left to himself, she was certain her father would have simply disposed of everything through a dealer. She wondered why he didn't. It occurred to her that it might be a sort of a test through which her father would be able to rank the worthiness of his offspring. She decided to ask for nothing, which seemed the safest course and the most virtuous, Cordelia-like. Win by losing. Never take the field. But in the end she changed her mind. It began to seem more satisfying to ask for something, one thing — the Lincoln — and see what he would do. In this way she could turn it around into a test of him instead of her. She didn't want the Lincoln per se, and she told him so in her letter. If it were hers she'd trade it in for something more practical, more to her taste. This, she realized, provided him with a graceful loophole through which to excuse himself if he wanted to give the car to her sister.

But the test results surprised her. It was she her father dispatched to Texas to acquire the car. She didn't know how it was that she had come to be the intended object of his benefi-cence — why not her half-sister, of whom he was much more fond, or her brother? She couldn't have predicted the unnerving-ness of finding herself favored. She wasn't certain in what ways she might now be obligated.

However, the ultimate disposition of the car remained unclear, vied for as it was not only by Louise's father but also by Marion's estranged adopted son, Kenny, and by Ella, Marion's nurse paramour, beneficiary of only a refrigerator and a leaf blower. At issue, to be decided by the First National Bank of Midland, executor of Marion's estate, was the definition of household goods — which were what had been bequeathed to Louise's father, as opposed to other sorts of assets — and whether the car should be included in that category.

In a preemptive move Louise's father had requested the use of the car in the interim while the will was probated and the bankers pondered. Mr. Swan had acceded and was now under the mistaken impression that Louise came as a courier and would deliver the Lincoln to her father in San Francisco for his own use. Her father — life's moral arbiter — apparently in this instance, to her surprise and in her behalf, didn't mind exerting himself in what Louise thought was an ethical gray area. Having wrested the car away from Ella, who had no claim on it except need, desire, and possession — she'd been driving it since Marion's death — he now wanted it for himself in order to bestow it upon Louise, and he wasn't willing to wait for it to be officially his to give or to risk that it wouldn't be.

Standing at the curb looking at the thrusting length of Detroit steel, Louise thought that perhaps there was, after all, a Lincoln driver buried within her. It looked like a lot of car. Stationary, it gave the appearance of momentum as if impetus lifted the nose and settled the weight down onto the rear tires. Mr. Swan held the door and Louise slid into an interior that smelled of leather and dust. Texans, she thought, expressed their wealth with an extravagance that retained the essence of its sources, cattle and oil. When Mr. Swan slipped behind the wheel she had to suppress an avid, proprietary impatience. She wanted to drive, to feel the leap of power.

Riding into Midland with Mr. Swan, trying to keep her true purpose from him, her collusion with her father, Louise thought of gunslingers, dangerous men recognizable by their reticence who hit town like a weather front, made a mockery of the guileless citizens, and blew out again, leaving havoc in their wake. "To the town of Amarillo rode a stranger one fine day/Didn't talk to folks around him, didn't have too much to say/No one dared to ask his business, no one dared to make a slip/For the stranger there among them wore a big iron on his hip/Big iron, big iron": Marty Robbin's tenor from some repository of memory wailing in her brain.

Mr. Swan wanted to know her past and her profession, the route she planned to travel and the duration of the journey. "Head west, I suppose," she said, "and see how long it takes. I haven't looked at a map." Her getaway as she thought of it — she wasn't going to San Francisco at all. She was aware that her laconic responses to his inquiries could be taken as evasive or haughty, might signal duplicity. She didn't think he meant to pry, he was only curious and was himself completely open. He'd come from San Angelo, he told her, pronouncing it as though it was one word, Sangelo, when the bank he worked for there closed, and he didn't like Midland, but he felt fortunate to have a job and went home on the weekends.

"There's a lot of money in Midland," he said. "Oil money. In Midland I can add a zero to any of the accounts I handled before." He smiled over at her, lobbing this confidence into her court like a service he expected her to return. Louise looked away and imagined reserve folding her up like a jackknife.

Midland was an oil town with nothing on the west Texas prairie to keep it from spreading, so it grew horizontally. The streets were wide and the buildings low. Everything was the same dun, the dun of the car, as though the surrounding earth had been leached of color, quarried for stone, gravel, and sand, mixed into cement and mortar, faced onto buildings. Nothing about it was familiar to Louise. She remembered it only vaguely as it had been when she visited as a child, residential streets of ranch houses set down in broad bleached yards of cheat grass, a town of people who called somewhere else home. Marion moved there from San Antonio with Faye, her father's sister, after the war and worked all the years since, until he retired, as a CPA for Texaco. Grandma followed them out in forty-nine and lived next door, a treacle calamity.

Louise was tired. She had taken a red-eye out of Seattle to save on the fare and had spent the night in the Las Vegas airport between planes without any sleep at all. She'd planned to put her bag in a locker and go in to the casinos, make an adventure of it, but in the end she hadn't found the heart for it. She'd played video poker on the concourse until her quarters ran out, then she'd sat up at the gate.

Mr. Swan wanted to buy her lunch. She was hungry and she thought she provided a diversion from his routine and that it was important to him to do the right thing by her. To decline would deny all of that, but fatigue and good nature might let down her guard. She didn't want to burden his conscience, and perhaps complicate her own plans, with a fuller understanding of the destiny of the Lincoln. She had other business in Midland, nothing she was looking forward to, and then she wanted to slide behind the wheel and blow out of town, head west, and maybe make El Paso.

Mr. Swan, Louise thought, knew there was something fishy going on, but he was too civil to press her so he decided to relinquish the car and ignore his suspicion. They parked in front of the bank while he read the odometer and noted down the mileage. Louise signed an informal letter acknowledging receipt of the car; then he was gone and she was alone. As she watched him walk into the bank she thought she'd never see him again. She was wrong, but at the time it seemed a little sad. He had won her with an essential gentlemanliness. He was Texan through and through.

Mr. Swan had told Louise how to reach the nursing home on the loop road that needlessly circled the city — planning for a distant future when the broad streets of town might clog with traffic — but she missed the exit and had to double back — a manifestation, she supposed, of dread.

She sat for a moment in the car in the parking lot before going in. This was a visit of obligation, performed for its own sake, for the sake of decorum.

Inside, it was like Midland itself, broad transverse corridors built to accommodate the passage of wheelchairs, and it was pleasant, as such places go.

Louise couldn't remember when she'd last seen her aunt — ten years ago, maybe more. Faye had been a stately woman with a heavy glossy braid of brown hair coiled on top of her head like a bird's nest or a crown, and a mouth full of scissored teeth. She had been an elementary school principal, the less favored child in a family that revered boys, blondes, and physicians. She sat now in a wheelchair, bound in place, hands limp in her lap, thinning hair completely white, looking vacantly out of the family eyes, blinking slowly at the world with a misleading serenity.

Louise thought of suicide, of the moment when you might recognize the onset of the decline, yet still have the wits to act. There could be no hesitation. You'd need a fatalist's nature. Pull the trigger before forgetting the reasons why.

She told Faye who she was. "Louise," she said, "Joyce's daughter," surprising herself with the choice of alliance, not claiming her father whose name Faye might more likely recognize, but invoking her mother from out of the past. Faye murmured and Louise imagined that she frowned slightly in an effort to concentrate as though some residual memory prompted her to attempt the expected response, like a child called on in class who feigned a struggle to recollect an answer that had never been known and could never be recalled. Then the effort, if there was one, was abandoned and Faye stared at Louise as a cat might, or a reptile, unflustered, inscrutable; she turned her head away, regal as a sovereign signaling that the audience was over.

Louise walked down the hall, past the nurses' station. It felt like school to her, as though she might be noticed and arrested, required to produce a hall pass. But there was no formality here. You were on your own. Once inside you could wander.

Louise thought her grandmother wasn't in her room. There was only a crumpled afghan of crocheted squares tossed on the bed. They'd taken her off somewhere or perhaps she'd died. A moment of relief. But when she looked closer, it was Hattie, a skeleton in a sack of skin lying beneath the blanket, grown so small she didn't dent the bed. Oh! Louise thought, the armature was so slight after the flesh was gone. She'd seen human bones before, in dioramas, reconstructed digs at the great museum of anthropology in Mexico City where people crowded against the rail, many deep, to stare mutely down on curled skeletons, knees to ribs and arms close like folded wings. But she wasn't prepared for this. This was worse than she had imagined.

"Grandma," Louise said. The sound of her own voice startled her. There was no response. "Grandma," she said again. Hattie's eyes were part way open, her mouth sagged. Louise didn't want to touch her, afraid she'd rattle into a heap like pick-up-sticks. She didn't know how to rouse her. She thought Hattie was dying at that moment, before her eyes. An eternity between each breath. Someone must be summoned.

She rang and after a very long time a big black woman came, an attendant, who was unconcerned. She shook Hattie fiercely and bellowed into her ear, "Miz Ayres! Miz Ayres! You got company here, Miz Ayres." Louise was horrified by her roughness, though she didn't seem unkind, and amazed that she didn't shake Grandma loose of life itself. "You've got to speak loud, ma'am," she said, "get their attention. They don't hear, you know, unless they want to. Stubborn that way." Hattie stirred into what apparently was wakefulness.

"Thank you," Louise said. She sat down and picked up the bones of her grandmother's hand, skin papery and cool as a lizard. Hattie's mind wandered. "Where's my baby?" she wailed. "Who's got my baby?" Her hand scrabbled in Louise's. Louise could not think of any possible way to answer. The attendant had gone out.

Love, she thought, a big empty space that allowed no entry except to the particular object of desire. What closer bond could there be than between mother and daughter? But Hattie emerged from the fog of senility only for her son, Louise's father, and only the presence of the now-departed Marion summoned back a vestige of Faye. It seemed to Louise a peculiarly female perversity, one that she shared, to invest some remote other with an arbitrary and unwished-for dominion over happiness. What stamina, and how foolish, to endure the endless torment of hope and longing (the thought of M. like an ice pick near her heart). Hattie and Faye, perambulated by robust young women, black or Spanish, who called them Honey and Sugar, for years had rolled on silent wheels past each other in the halls, like ships in the night, unaware. Wouldn't their eyes have met one day, recognition blossomed? They might have fallen into each other's arms with cries of reunion, found solace just down the hall. But their eyes were like the doors of storage lockers, rolled down and staring blankly out at a meaningless present while behind in the dark the rich confusion of life lay jumbled.

Now Hattie's eyes rolled in her head, aiming off in different directions, milky and opaque. The eyes themselves could perhaps still see but the brain had abandoned the effort. She didn't have her teeth in. Louise supposed there was no need and possibly some danger. Grandma was one hundred years old. What kept her clinging so tenaciously to life?

Louise let her drift back into sleep or coma. Louise's own grip on life had never been so strong, and it seemed to her that

64

rousing Hattie distressed her to no purpose. Sleep — death — was preferable. Louise watched her breathe, thinking that each inhalation would be her last. She thought of the boundary where she was poised like an invisible precipice or barrier, the interface between two states of being, like opposing currents in water or air. Slight and meaningless as her life now was, reduced to breathing and elusive fragments of unintelligible thought, still it was life. In a moment or a day (or as it turned out, in a week) the mystery that was Grandma would slip through the boundary and return no more.

Across the hall a woman's voice suddenly called, "Oh, God!" like a jolt of electricity. "Please send someone! Oh, God, won't you send someone?" Blasts of the summoning buzzer accompanied the shouting and the commotion flooded the corridor. Louise jumped up and went to the door and looked up and down the hallway. No one was running to respond. It sounded like an emergency but apparently was only a routine lament. The woman shouted for her children, for Jesus, for God to come down, show himself, and take her away, relieve her of loneliness. It was Mrs. Pearl, Louise discovered when an attendant finally came and addressed her by name in the dark syrup of Southern black English, impatient but not unkind. But Mrs. Pearl wanted more than an attendant, she wanted God himself and all her children to appear before her and carry her home. She shouted on.

Louise wandered around the room. In her grandmother's room, as in others she'd glimpsed as she walked down the hall, a few pieces of ornate mahogany futilely endeavored to maintain continuity with a past existence, achieving instead a poignant suggestion of divestment. Remnants from a shipwreck.

Framed on the wall were Faye's high school graduation portrait in sepia — Faye, never pretty, but young and smiling then — and a book jacket photo of Louise's father blown up disconcertingly to nearly life-size. An Avedon, each pore and electric eyebrow hair revealed.

On the dresser, accelerating the passage of time, condensing life, telescoping it into a few captured moments, a series of albums sent on subsequent Christmases by Louise's sister chronicled each year's events in family snapshots. Like a flip book or the instant before drowning, your life flashing past.

Louise couldn't catch her breath. There was a fist in her chest. She closed the door. If she sobbed aloud, a nurse might hear, offer comfort, mistake distress for grief. She saw too much of herself in these old women. It wasn't that she would one day come to this, it was to already be there, to realize that it was only hope and illusion, nothing tangible or real, that separated her from them. They were wailing, babbling women, beloved of nobody, calling out for departed husbands and lovers, for absent children, for God, bereft and inconsolable. Mrs. Pearl could beseech as she might, God wasn't listening, there was no plan and no salvation.

There was no way to know how long to stay, when to go, no ritual of departure to observe. She had only to make up her mind, turn her back and leave.

Louise bought cigarettes at a mini-mart on the outskirts of town, something she'd promised herself not to do, but by now it never even occurred to her not to. She would have had a drink as well but there were three hundred miles to cover on an empty stomach and no sleep if she wanted to make El Paso. Hope was already reasserting itself in the belief that she could outrun despair, distance herself from truth. Out past Odessa she pulled to the side of the road and changed into her blue jeans, standing in the shelter of the passenger side door. The Lincoln shuddered in the wake of a passing truck.

There was country, gospel, and Spanish on the radio but her kids had surmised there'd be a tape player in the Lincoln and had slipped Bruce Springsteen into her briefcase. With the volume turned up loud, the wind and road noise sealed away, Louise heard every lyric of "Tunnel of Love" as she chased the sun into a protracted setting, hurtling across the curve of the earth. Texas was a big and vacant state to be in.

In El Paso, at a package store in a strip mall just off the highway, Louise bought a fifth of Jim Beam after checking into a motel. It was dark by then and she was chilled by an unexpected bitter wind chasing around the parking lot. "Texas," she said to the cashier, "I thought it'd be warm."

"Wrong, sweetheart," he croaked, his voice startling her. He talked through a hole in his throat, vibrations mechanically translated by a box he held against his windpipe. "Antifreeze," he said about the bottle. "Thin your blood, keep you from seizing up."

She smiled. "Let's hope," she said. But something lodged in her own throat, the endearment or the idea of herself inert as a frozen engine block. Or the further reminder of frailty and decay. She could hear him sucking air behind her as she left and she wanted to run.

Caffeine and cigarettes had erased her appetite and the whiskey was going to hit like a roundhouse, but she couldn't imagine venturing out again into the dark in search of a meal.

In the breezeway she filled a plastic ice bucket, then went back to her room. She wished she could talk to her boys, but it was too late to call. The darkness and cold stretched the distance between Seattle and her Texas motel room to galactic proportions. Home was as distant as Pluto. No one knew where she was. She couldn't be reached.

Her circumstances seemed like something out of fiction or cinema, a woman on the run risking capture for a few hours sleep, the getaway car camouflaged outside against an adobe wall. But she'd come in late or missed the first chapters. What was going on?

A friend, traveling light, tore his books in half along the spines, and sometimes in half again, to make them more portable. His shelves were full of stories with no beginnings or no ends, interrupted journeys, adventures lacking context. Reading became like life, inconclusive, baffling.

She poured a drink and ran a tub. Gratitude for the prosaic luxury of hot water. In the fluorescent light of the bathroom a stranger stared out of the mirror at Louise. It was a subtle transformation, one that would pass any but the most exacting scrutiny. At various times in her life she'd had the conviction that her mother, or later her husband, had been replaced by a counterfeit. A gap behind the bicuspid when her mother smiled, a glint of gold. Anyone less vigilant would have missed the substitution. Louise kept the secret to herself. Now, the same phenomenon befell her. The face in the mirror looked similar, but inauthentic. She couldn't say exactly how. It wasn't anything she could put her finger on, she simply knew it, though inside she felt the same as always. Louise smiled to disarm the decoy and brushed its teeth as though they were her own.

The possibility of waking at three in the morning, uncertain of who she was, and the mental grope backwards in search of chronology until she came upon Grandma and the nursing home, were too horrible to risk. Two valiums washed down with a glass of watered whiskey swallowed the night.

In the morning when she woke a splinter of light split the drapes. It was late. She could smell the bourbon left in the glass on the night table, sweet as ether, and stale cigarette smoke caught in her hair.

She stood at the window and gazed out over Interstate 10 to the Rio Grande, channeled at that point between concrete levees, and beyond, to the Third World. At first she didn't know what she was seeing, or didn't see it because it was so at variance with what her eye expected — at first it looked like bare desert hills, dusty gray under the pale morning sun — but the hills were covered with shacks, hovels of mud and corrugated tin, thousands of them blending into the landscape like a prairie dog town or an ant hill, a warren of human habitation. North of the freeway to the west towered the high rise buildings of the University of Texas. U-TEP, they called it. It seemed implausible that the thread of river kept the sides from mingling.

It was appealing in its way, Louise thought, the Mexican side, the camouflaged aspect of those thousands of dwellings, as though the inhabitants lived in closer harmony with the land, but appalling too, the distance compressed into those few hundred yards.

In Mexico, Louise thought, anything was possible. On a February day in the nineteen-fifties, just across the river in Ciudad Juarez, some money changed hands and Louise's father dissolved sixteen years of marriage. She had the documents from among her mother's papers, long filmy pages typed twice, once in English and again in Spanish, a notarized affidavit swearing the translation was accurate, a statement from the vice-consul of the United States of America disclaiming responsibility for the validity of the other documents. Lies bound together on blue paper, seals and ribbons giving an appearance of festivity and authority, declaring her

69

father a resident of the Bravos District of the State of Chihuahua and granting him a divorce from her mother. Louise imagined him, a troubled young physician, leaving a cheap motel on the El Paso side, crossing the river under the morning sun, and returning that evening transformed, divested of history and responsibility.

Louise too had been to Mexico. She'd been across the border as a child, to Nogales with her mother and then again more recently. Mexico had meaning for her; its proximity bent her thoughts south like a magnet. It was, she thought, like looking at the face of a triumphant rival. It cowed and fascinated, vanquished her to the pallid north.

She thought perhaps she would drive across, negotiate the bridge and maneuver the Lincoln through the streets of Juarez, find a highway and sweep south, sleep on pool tables or locked in the back seat if she couldn't find a hotel. They'd fall at her feet when they saw her fair hair and the four hundred caballos under her hood. She'd adopt the customs and eat men's hearts.

In her mind she followed red lines leading south like veins to Mexico City.

eight

IN THE AIRPORT of Mexico City, where she'd been the year before, she had been reminded of times when she was a child and first traveled by air, shunted across the continent between parents in the days when you still disembarked onto the tarmac, and of the shock and dislocation upon arrival of stepping into a new and strange atmosphere, an assault of warmth or humidity or scent. You couldn't prepare for it.

On the concourse, stationed along the walls, uniformed boys stood guard, rifle butts braced against their thighs. An image of a fracas presented itself involuntarily, shots echoing in the low-ceilinged space so she couldn't determine their source, her cheek pressed against the cold tiles as she lay prone behind a column. Orderliness and logic were left behind, expediency reigned.

She muddled through the daunting procedures of customs, changing money and purchasing a chit for a taxi to the hotel. Friends in Seattle had told her how to do this and what to expect. People at home thought variously that she was gallant or foolish to travel alone. They didn't know why she was going.

She was isolated by her lack of Spanish. A foreigner, she thought, like an idiot or a madman talking gibberish, was released from the constraints of convention. Unable to communicate, you were less guarded. Traveling, you might unearth an essential self, who you were at heart.

Outside, the city was unnaturally gloomy, portentous beneath a canopy of smog as though just before a storm or following a fire or an explosion, air heavy with particulates, thick enough to chew. And the cars, the appalling disrepair of the cars, the narrow lanes of the freeway, the cavalier disregard of the drivers — Louise was wide-eyed with astonishment. At home safety was legislated. This wouldn't be allowed.

Her taxi whipped around in the traffic, passing turquoise and pink tenements strung with washing, peeling billboards she couldn't read. It was rush hour and a long drive to Chapultapec Park, but it didn't matter to Louise because M. was shooting and wouldn't be at the hotel until the early hours of the morning when he would come to her.

The hotel, when she got there, was equally foreign in its opulence, a vertical palace at the end of the Paseo de la Reforma, an obelisk from another culture set down like a visiting spacecraft. They spoke English at the desk.

An impostor, Louise thought, experiences simultaneously the thrill of deception and the fear of disclosure. And secrets confer power. She was no ordinary tourist, her business in Mexico City was clandestine. She was an interloper in the corridor on M.'s floor, looking over her shoulder, fearing a maid or an American guest who would know her for what she was.

She wrote her room number on the back of a postcard and slipped it under his door. As they'd arranged. Too risky to share a room. His name, her room number, her initial. She wondered if he would keep the card, a memento, conceal it from his wife among innocuous letters and receipts and come across it years later with a rush of memory. She thought not.

She had hours to wait during which there was nothing to do with herself. Too late for sightseeing and no companion for dinner. In her room she might be anywhere. Downstairs it was the same. It could be Tokyo or London. For M. there was no romance to shooting in Mexico, only difficulties. People got sick and bored. They complained about the food and the altitude and the weather. The luxury hotel was a compensation, an approximation of Los Angeles to appease the cast and crew.

Louise went out and walked for a while. Night had fallen. There was no street life here in this part of the city, only darkened office buildings, the park, and the boulevard, a river of traffic passing beside her.

Later, in her room, anticipation made her wakeful. She drank brandy and hoped for sleep.

A tap at her door just before dawn. She flew across the room. The instant silent fusion before the door had even closed behind him that dispensed with greetings and awkwardness, plunged directly to fierce communion of lips and tongues and breath, his hands upon her, sliding over the silk of her nightgown. The back of his shirt was damp with sweat like a working man's, his body more frail than before, his face thinner between her hands. In the dark there was a glint of light on eyes and teeth when he drew back and smiled, breathless.

The day spent behind closed blinds. No sense of time.

In the Zona Rosa Louise drank a glass of wine and waited out a cloudburst. "Vino blanco" even she could say. The waiters unfurled awnings overhead. People ran for shelter. A woman in a red dress, pitched forward from the waist, hurried on stiletto heels under cover of a newspaper held by her escort, her elbow gripped in his hand. His gallantry rendered him foolish, arms contorted, legs scissoring. Louise preferred a man who wouldn't even hold the door.

Afternoon thundershowers were common in high altitude basins during the summer months. Earlier, from her room in the hotel, she'd seen the clouds building and the rain moving southward toward the city. From the perspective of the thirty-first floor the low buildings of the city, the miles of shanties spreading away to the distant rim of hills, had the aspect of a plain. Louise was reminded of home, the plains of her youth.

Negative ions in the atmosphere, it was said, which accompanied an electrical storm, were cheering. She was, for the moment, happy. Still, to be in Mexico was a surprise, and under these circumstances it defied description, like an out-of-body experience. She didn't feel she was in possession of her own life; more as though she were a character in someone else's fiction, impelled by another's imagination.

She wished M. had asked her to go with him somewhere outside the city where he was scouting for the red hills of Mars. Instead, she had looked at bones and murals like an ordinary tourist and at the rooms in Frida Kahlo's blue house in Coyoacan where there were hardly any other visitors. It felt like a home more than a museum, and occupied, as though its inhabitants were only out for the moment and would soon be back, proposing drinks in the garden. She looked at the bed where Frida had lain and at her painted plaster cast which exactly described the dimensions of the rib cage which had contained her heart. A perverse shrine to passion and suffering

The rain moved south. The waiters rolled up the awnings. Louise paid, inspecting the unfamiliar coins, and then she walked, gazing into shop windows, trying to remember the sizes and interests of her boys, but they had dimmed and become theoretical, like someone else's children, and the tooled leather, T-shirts, silver, and weavings they might have liked had no appeal for her. Instead, she bought cigarettes in the same familiar pack, but with the copy printed in Spanish. Then she flagged a taxi.

Afterwards, she thought, you couldn't say when you knew. You imagined you remembered omens and uneasiness. You collected knowledge with unknown senses, but discounted it until words gave it weight.

On a Saturday night the marble lobby of the Nikko echoed with festivity. Here people dressed for dinner (she saw a tuxedo in the elevator). A band playing in the lounge. The tattoo of women's high heels rattling like castanets, and laughter. No one was alone. It was Saturday night, full of potential, there were hours ahead during which anything could happen.

They were going to dinner with others, a necessity, M. had said, that couldn't be avoided and Louise must be very careful. He had explained her as an acquaintance, a writer doing research in Mexico City. Louise didn't mind. She welcomed the appearance in his world, a child allowed to sit with the grownups, stay up late, suck the bourbon from the cherries left at the bottoms of the manhattan glasses.

She saw them as she crossed the lobby. A screenwriter and his wife, the writer's agent and M., suddenly unfamiliar in a suit and a public face. Louise had looked forward to the charade of shaking his hand in front of strangers, deception rendering the mundane erotic, but he didn't offer it. He only nodded at her and she thought he was too curt.

She knew immediately from their slight condescension and perfunctory interest that she was dismissed as inconsequential. It wasn't troubling to her — was, in fact, a relief, for she could disappear. There would be no burden of curiosity placed upon her, no vigilance required. She wondered, though; had M. shrugged and rolled his eyes in wordless complaint of her presence? Perhaps they credited him now with some sort of misdirected good will. Such a nice guy, people take advantage.

In the cab she sat in back, squeezed between M. and the agent, shoulder to shoulder, thigh against thigh. She felt like the moon, warm on one side only. They talked across and around her and there wasn't the slightest surreptitious pressure from M.'s side to reassure her. She might well have been a stranger. She kept her hands clasped in her lap, her eyes forward. Her spirits were deflating. This was harder than she had imagined.

They ate in a colonial hacienda renovated into a French restaurant, but Louise had no appetite. She would have preferred a reckless tamale from a street vendor. M. leaned over and asked if her dinner was all right. "It's fine, thank you," she said, annoyed. Not once had his knee touched hers beneath the table or their eyes met with any meaning. The talk flowed around her without her participation. Talk of the production, gossip, anecdotes — versions of stories he'd told her in private, for her ears only, she'd thought — plus names she knew or thought she ought to know, names she'd never heard. She tried to think of what she'd say if she were what she pretended to be. Normally, she wasn't shy. This was a window onto his world, into the social congress of his everyday life, something she'd never share. She felt relegated to the status of a wife — the same invisibility but none of the privilege.

She left the table and went to the bathroom and stayed a while. He would think she was sick, but she wasn't, only bored and sad. In the mirror she admired the neckline of her dress, the arc of her collarbone, and the hollow of her throat. She didn't wear any jewelry except an onyx ring that had been her mother's. She was the only person she knew who had never pierced her ears. In all the time she'd known him, by now nearly two years, she wasn't certain M. had noticed any of these things. Her face crumpled and she began to cry. The attendant holding towels was watching. Louise took one and mopped her face. "Un hombre," she said but the woman might have been deaf or carved from stone. Louise gave her a handful of pesos without counting as she left. She wondered if she was drunk and tried to count the glasses of wine backwards to the first one in the Zona Rosa. But it wasn't that; she was as steady as Gibraltar in her heels.

Back at the hotel the others wanted to go to the disco. Louise thought they hoped that M.'s celebrity, or the star's, if he were there, would rub off like gilt onto them; they'd go home enhanced.

They went up an unmarked back stairway guarded by a gendarme who patted down the men in the party ahead of them and inspected the women's handbags. Would people be carrying drugs or weapons, then? It seemed commonplace to M. She realized he would have been there before; he'd been at the Nikko for weeks, a reminder of his life without her. Inside, it was a metal cavern, disorienting as a hall of mirrors. Video images and strobes of light bounced wildly off the aluminum walls, distorting space. Lit smoke appeared solid, like walking into fur. You couldn't talk, or even think, and the only way you'd know you were in Mexico was no one wanted ice in the drinks.

They were too early. The band didn't start until midnight. M. went interminably to the men's room. Louise drank warm bourbon and wondered if he were sick or if it could be cocaine that kept him there. Anything was possible. People got weird on location. She'd come to the wrong party; she could see that now. She wished she hadn't come at all. She wished she'd stayed behind, ordered up, or gone out by herself. The company was inane. She was afraid that the pulsing lights would trigger a headache and couldn't imagine wanting to dance here. She'd pictured something else, a slow dance in M.'s arms, a tango with a rose in her teeth. She was losing herself. The charade had become reality. They were strangers, really, barely known to each other.

When M. came back he wanted to leave. He didn't want to wait it out until the band started.

Louise fell on the steps down to the exit door. The disco was like a deprivation tank — you lost your depth perception, your balance, couldn't tell up from down — and she missed a stair in the dark. The agent grabbed her arm to help her up. M. had walked on ahead.

They all rode up in the elevator together. Louise's floor came first. "I'll call you," M. said in front of the others and Louise's heart turned over, though they wouldn't know that he meant then, that night, within moments. It was like a bedroom farce, she thought, full of stealth and stupidity.

When he came to her room he was quiet. He lay on his back looking into space.

"What's wrong?" she asked.

"Nothing."

"Something is," she said. Someone's cold hand was squeezing her heart.

When he told her she thought maybe she had known all along, even before she arrived in Mexico, something in his voice on the telephone that she might have interpreted if she'd been more alert. It was Lina, a Mexican girl. "She's stolen a hair or a button," he said, "I'm not myself. She's using special powers." Louise laughed. The absurdity of it. Nothing that she could combat.

Later, she imagined it as a film and herself as a minor player, a walk-on in Lina's story. Sides, they called it when actors got only pages, not the whole script, just the scenes where they appeared, to economize perhaps, save a tree. She was peripheral, set dressing. When she walked off, the camera wouldn't follow.

From things he said, tiny clues, scraps of information, like imagining a dinosaur from a single bone, Louise constructed scenes, assembled plot and character.

A twenty-four-year-old Mexican stunt girl, a face of copper planes, torso flat and long, inner thighs hollow from horseback, bowed for love, more Aztec than Spanish. She blazed with anger. Two years earlier an American gaffer had broken his promises and abandoned her. She lived now in poverty in her grandmother's house in the southern part of the city and slept on the floor beside the American's bastard son, no wiser but more cunning. She had caught a glimpse of what was possible, rumors of gold to the north, like Coronado's city, and she believed she knew how to get there. Lina had dreams and powers. Her father was a toreador, her grandmother a witch, or so she said. She had a fire in her belly. Black eyes looked out of her Indian face and waited for opportunity. She was a bandit lying in ambush for a gringo savior.

Mexico City's was an unhealthy atmosphere. An inversion system overhead trapped smog and emanations from the swamp the city was built on. You could imagine ancient uneasy spirits too, virgins with severed heads and homesick skeletons rattling inside Spanish armor, not dispersed but remaining captive, circulating in the stagnant air, bartering their powers among the inhabitants. You got down into Mexico and reason slipped away like a snake's skin. You began to believe in spells and magic, pagan gods that for a lamb or a virgin would bestow eternal youth or the gift of sorcery.

Louise thought it was a pitfall of location shooting, the boredom and intensity, nothing mysterious. It happened all the time. But M. believed in magic. As a child he'd believed in alchemy and levitation until he learned the magician's tricks. He didn't believe in love, but he hoped for some yet undiscovered mystery, a power to submit to. He hoped for miracles. In Lina he thought he'd found one. He held her gently, like a daughter, and fiercely, a witch in his arms. He saw Lina in candlelight bent over his photograph, murmuring incantations, swelling like a released genie, engulfing him.

He costumed her garishly in a spiky orange wig and a chartreuse Lycra dress with the straps pulled down to display her shoulders, and filmed her gut shot, a punk victim. A wire snapped to a harness under her dress yanked her backwards to mime the impact and a charge in front exploded a capsule of blood across her belly. She had to prepare by not preparing, a contradiction, knowing the jerk would come, and knowing when, seeing the chalk mark coming as she strutted. She had to be rag-doll ready. When it came her head snapped downward and her arms flew out in an involuntary gesture of supplication.

Louise imagined the disbelief when Lina first felt M.'s eyes upon her, and the first cautious stirrings of hope, dismissed immediately. Lina would not have sought opportunity in such exalted spheres. She had an easy fraternity with the grips, electricians, and the second echelon of actors, they were possibilities within her grasp. The special effects man who rigged her harness laughed at her flat breasts and flicked her nipple with his thumb. Lina didn't care. But M.'s eyes returned and with them came the giddy elation of certainty. Her eyes flashed and she danced a flamenco in swirling skirts. An exchange of glances, a flurry, and confidence settled upon her. Now she would wait. His advance would come.

She told her boyfriend, Guillermo, but he didn't believe her. "Bring me an ear," he said, biting hers, "like the Getty hostage. Then I'll believe it." Lina giggled. Guillermo had no fear of sharing her, his co-conspirator. Their alliance was deeper than sex, more binding than matrimony. They had cold criminal greed in common, and cannibalism in their Aztec blood. Opportunists, like antler ferns, they would feed on bodies to get where they were going.

They made love parked in an alley, hot with potential, on top of a blanket spread on the floorboards of his Impala where the back seat had once been. A life of ease swam before their eyes — pools and malls, Mercedes Benzes and rock and roll. Guillermo's breath smelled of beer, a cross of silver alloy dangled from a verdigris line around his neck, and his stomach was flat and hard, knotted with muscle. In his mind a roll of hundreds occupied his pocket like a hard-on. Guillermo whispered into Lina's ear perversions that the gringo would expect, and she laughed.

Love, for them, was hot and quick.

When the door closed behind M. there was nothing left of Louise. All she was in Mexico was M.'s dream and he was no longer dreaming her. She vanished.

She pictured the lighted square of her window seen from outside, part of a random pattern, and thought about how you'd wonder if you looked up from the sidewalk below about the lives going on in those rooms. You could imagine whole lives for hotel guests in the same way you used to create worlds for the travelers whipping past on passenger trains. Louise tried to imagine herself, a silhouette against the lighted pane, an Anglo woman smoking a cigarette at the window on the thirty-first floor in the small hours of the night.

Her armor was tarnished and she carried her banners furled, but her legs too knew the feel of a horse and she had a thousand miles behind her. She knew the terrain. Lina might swing up behind M.'s saddle, but Louise would ride alongside. She could cast no spells but would hold him in the vise of patience. She was easier to summon than to banish.

nine

BUT WHEN LOUISE left the motel in El Paso she got back onto
I-10 and headed west after all. In Mexico, if she crossed the
bridge and nosed south out of Juarez, she might lose herself,
turn up an arroyo, sweep her tire tracks out behind her, and sit
down to desiccate in the spidery shade of an ocotillo. Never
come home.

She liked the Lincoln. It was made for the road, made for
Texas where petroleum was plentiful and the highways
stretched out to infinity straight as string. It wasn't a car she
would ever have thought of buying for herself, it didn't reflect
her, whoever she thought herself to be, but its excess released
her from herself. Behind the wheel she became someone else,
a well-heeled Texan, assured, caroming down the highway,
entitled to a big share of the road. She put El Paso in her
rearview mirror, Grandma and Faye behind her. The Lincoln's
nose was pointed west and she headed for Los Angeles.

She was stopped at an immigration checkpoint on the New
Mexico line. She turned off the engine and got out to open the
trunk for the officer. He watched her curiously. It was empty.
Carpeted and big enough for a whole family of aliens. She
walked away to the edge of the road and looked at the sky.
High up the wind was pulling mares' tails east like taffy.

She hadn't accustomed herself to the car. She'd gotten in
and gotten underway without adjusting the mirrors, left the
seat the way she'd found it — Mr. Swan must have driven with
his arms and legs sticking straight out. She'd forgotten there'd
be a button to pop the trunk.

She turned her back to the wind and lit a cigarette. The
officer was still watching her. A lady didn't smoke on her feet,
she'd learned that as a girl. She walked back to the car and slid

in. He touched his hat as she pulled away. It was something about the car, its mass and self-importance insulating her like a fur.

Louise tried to mentally erase the interstate, see the landscape as it had been when you crossed the desert under cover of darkness with a canvas water bottle slung from your radiator cap and a rooster tail of dust a ghost on your heels, when the country was full of promise and peril and her mother was a girl and Reeve Deason was a wildcatter.

Sometimes she imagined she was Reeve Deason's daughter, that he'd impregnated her mother somehow with his spirit so that she carried his legacy along with her own father's genes. She had photographs her mother had kept, tiny faded photographs with deckled edges showing a man in a slouch hat and jodhpurs standing on braced legs in front of an oil well, the wooden mast crude and spectral against the prairie, all of Texas at his back. Flash floods laced the draws on summer nights and Reeve kept gin and a pistol in his glove box.

It was the pistol that changed her mother's mind, or the gin. Perhaps he took a swing at her. Louise didn't know. Her mother didn't marry him but she didn't forget him either.

Years later her mother went back to Texas. She took the kids and traveled south, leaving their father behind in Massachusetts. It was a trial separation, though Louise didn't know it at the time. She believed the public version — that it was for her own health, to allow the hot desert air to cure her pneumonia like another generation's tuberculosis prescription. They left at the end of her first-grade year. Louise felt frail and significant, a rare blown egg. Inside the thin shell of her chest she imagined her lung shriveled like a deflated balloon. Adults looked at her with worried eyes and touched her forehead with the backs of their fingers. But she exerted the power of her infirmity cautiously, wary of the withdrawal of indulgence.

During her turns in the front seat Louise had thrust her arm
out the window into the slipstream of unfamiliar air, her hand
stretched into a shape she imagined as a migratory bird, her
fingers and thumb flapping wings, while inside her head Tex
Ritter wailed, "My heart knows what the wild goose
knows/and I must go where the wild goose goes/Wild goose,
brother goose, which is best/A wandering foot or a heart at
rest?" It was a rhetorical question, the implication clear.
Louise imagined herself winging southward alone under her
own power.

They drove through Kentucky to see the thoroughbreds,
Nashua and Native Dancer, then crossed the Mississippi at
Memphis, and crawled across the immensity of Texas where
the grandmothers lived. They saw the caverns at Carlsbad, the
painted desert and the petrified forest, the Grand Canyon and
the ruins at Mesa Verde. Louise's nose bled on every mountain
pass as though altitude attenuated already delicate membranes.
Creeping up Oak Creek Canyon behind a tanker, Louise's
head tilted back, an ice cube pressed to the bridge of her nose
melting across her cheeks like tears, and the taste of blood in
her throat, her mother told a story of a nitroglycerin truck and
its driver — Yves Montand in *Wages of Fear*. Louise imagined
the driver preternaturally sensitive to the hazard of every
pebble beneath his tires, like the princess and the pea, a
perpetual frisson of dread.

At Nogales they crossed into Mexico. A black horse lay
outstretched beside the road, its belly ballooning like an enormous fig. Louise wouldn't believe it was dead. She thought it
was sick or injured and she pleaded to turn back.

They rented an apartment in Tucson and three days a week
her mother took Louise to a stable on the outskirts of town and
let her ride out into the desert among mesquite trees and dry
washes. Even chaperoned Louise pictured herself a lone

cowboy. She fell in love with a bad-tempered pinto and a dark sullen boy named Gene, though she thought his name was spelled Jean, like a girl, who saddled the mare with averted eyes and barely spoke to her. Louise thought she detected a wild kindred spirit, and she imagined he was mistreated, cruelly beaten in an empty stall at night for offenses he didn't commit, and that in daylight he proudly hid his tears and pain. Like the dead horse in Mexico, he only awaited the wand of her ministrations. Between the pinto and the boy Louise returned from her rides in a fever, cheeks flushed, eyes glassy and circled with fatigue. Her mother made her rest in a darkened room through the heat of the afternoon while downstairs in the yard outside her brother ran through a sprinkler.

While Louise rode her mother drank coffee in the stable office with Pete, the owner, and on Saturday nights a babysitter came. At home in Massachusetts Louise's father was sleeping with the woman who would become his second wife.

But when her mother proposed that they stay, keep the apartment and attend school in Tucson, Louise's renegade spirit folded its wings in terror. She could not face a schoolroom full of strangers. She cried and her mother yielded.

They were nearly home when Louise's mother downshifted on a rain-slick hill and went into a spin that took out a stretch of guardrail, crumpling two fenders and bending the frame.

The boy from San Antonio that Louise's mother had married instead of Reeve, the playwright in rumpled white linen and a halo of cigarette smoke, had renounced the theatre, entered medical school, enlisted in the Navy, served in the Pacific, and transmogrified into a New England psychiatrist who embellished Freud with his own Calvinist roots. No secret was safe from him. Dark impulses governed ordinary events, things were never as they seemed, behavior was an encrypted message from internal demons. He was like an inquisitor, you couldn't challenge his divination, and his tests, like drowning witches, defied reason, required capitulation. By his lights it wasn't an accident that her mother had had on a rainy afternoon in upstate New York. Conflict totaled the Oldsmobile, ambivalence swung the old blue whale around and slammed it into the guard rail.

Like a pioneer on the journey west winnowing his load as the oxen weakened, discarding pieces of his old life as circumstances tempered sentiment, Louise's father followed his mistress to California and left Louise and her mother behind. A bureau beside the Oregon trail.

Years later they drifted west again, to Wyoming this time. Louise's mother had located Reeve in Casper but Louise didn't know if she called, if they ever saw each other. She had never asked. But her mother wore dresses that summer, Louise remembered, that she sewed herself. Yards of printed cotton running through the machine, the smell of hot wires in the pedal and smoldering threads burned off with the tip of her cigarette, a beer and an ashtray always at her elbow. She whacked off her bun with her sewing scissors and her chestnut hair swung back into the pageboy of her youth. It was a different household then — loose hair, full skirts, the windows open in the evenings, June bugs thumping against the screens, heat lightning playing along the horizon. But Louise buttoned herself into damp blue jeans and drove her Plymouth into town; if her mother had a beau she never laid eyes on him.

Louise called Casper information once herself after her mother died, but there was no listing for Reeve. Perhaps she was too late or he might be in some other oil town, in Kansas or Oklahoma or drilling in the North Sea, twenty-one on and twenty-one off and the platform dry. There was no gin in the North Sea.

In the El Paso white pages there were two Deasons, but no Reeve. She'd looked. She'd looked for her own first boyfriend too, something she did sometimes in strange cities, bored and alone in a hotel room. There was one Victor Gallegos, but the phone was answered in Spanish and she said, "Sorry," and hung up, wondering, if she found him, if there'd be anything left they'd recognize in each other.

He'd been a thin boy with big eyes and a hawk nose, a gentle nature behind a fierce profile. Winter nights they went rabbit hunting, a gang of them with twenty-twos and a case of Coors, zig-zagging across the prairie in her Plymouth, rifles out all the windows, heater and radio blasting. With the evening bounce they picked up KOMA, Oklahoma City, fifty thousand watts of power, Buddy Holly and the Shirelles. They spot-lighted jack rabbits with a hand-held headlamp rigged to the battery. In Fort Collins the carcasses sold for fifty cents apiece for the pelts and the paws. Someone took the car the next day while Louise was in class and drove down with a trunk full of frozen rabbits. On good nights they made their beer money and then some.

Vic lived alongside the Southern Pacific tracks on the outskirts of Laramie, a pulled engine dangling like a lynch victim from a limb of a cottonwood in the bare yard in front of the house. He flipped the leaf springs on Louise's Plymouth to give it a rake and glued Mickey Mouse white walls onto the tires one afternoon in the school parking lot while she watched from the window during geometry, modifications that conferred a Latino élan.

The summer she got married, Vic pulled her over on the highway north of Laramie. She hadn't seen him for a while and didn't know who it was at first and was alarmed when he drew alongside in a construction company pickup, easing closer until her wheels were on the shoulder and she had to slow down and stop. They stood in the grass of the barrow pit and talked. He'd been in a fight since she'd seen him, had his front teeth knocked out with a tire iron. He said the bridge bothered him, but he pulled it out of his shirt pocket and put it in on her account. He was working on the interstate that was going in west of town. It was a warm afternoon with thunderheads building to the north over Elk Mountain. Louise showed him the chip of a diamond from Elliot on her fourth finger and told him she was getting married and felt with him the pang she expected the news would cause. He'd taken it hard when they broke up.

"A college boy," he said.

"Yes," she answered. It was the gulf that had kept them apart, more unbridgeable in imagination than it would have had to have been. He took her hand and laced his knobby brown fingers into hers, his palm hard and dry as warm cement.

Lives were shaped in unimaginable ways, Louise thought, every juncture freighted with consequence. Every life was a record of historical accident, a fingerprint of choice and chance. She was a casualty of fortune, as though through a chain of circumstance she had mistakenly come to be the wrong person. She'd be at home now, the saguaro familiar on the horizon, if her mother had married Reeve.

Louise hit Phoenix just as it was getting dark. Coming in from the east on Highway 60, she jogged around on broad palm-lined boulevards trying to find the interstate. She had cut north out of Lordsburg in New Mexico, intending to take 666 through the mountains, but she'd turned around at Clifton. There was road work ahead on the two-lane highway and a ranger told her to expect long delays. Even so, she had trouble making up her mind. She wanted to take the route, see the country, visit a weaver a friend had told her about, but she was daunted by the prospect of darkness, strangers, and the unwieldy car on tortuous turns. It was hard to make a decision alone with only her own wishes to consult. She parked on the shoulder and smoked a cigarette. There was no hurry, no one was waiting, though M. knew she was coming.

He was back from Mexico, cutting the picture in Los Angeles. Lina, he told Louise, made a mistake when she requisitioned for money. "Like a prostitute?" he'd asked. Louise could see his face, suddenly interested, alert. He gave her a thousand dollars and Lina went home in triumph, delivering the ear, she thought, the future assured. But the cloak of magic had frayed. M. admired a practical girl, but what could be purchased diminished in value.

High up, a vulture rode the thermals. Louise watched it soar. She would, she decided, abandon the scenic detour. She turned the car around and meandered toward Phoenix on secondary highways, stuck behind trucks and afraid to pass. Now she was unaccountably in a hurry and wished she'd stayed on I-10.

Phoenix ended abruptly to the west and the desert began. Louise was tired and low on gas. It seemed like a long time and little westward progress since she'd left El Paso. At Buckeye she filled the tank. On the map she'd taken it for a town, but it was only a junction, and the single motel was a bleak stucco row out in the darkness beyond the truck stop's glow.

The room didn't have a phone and there was a spider in the metal shower stall when she pulled the plastic curtain aside. She could have caught it on the end of a broom and shaken it out the door, but she was afraid to kill it or wash it down the drain. She thought about putting her clothes back on and complaining at the desk but she was afraid of the girl who had rented her the room, too. She'd looked mean and practical, like she did a business on the side turning tricks for the truckers. She'd step on the spider with her bare heel or catch it in her hand to torment Louise.

Louise gave up on a shower and slid between cold sheets and lay in the darkness, imagining catastrophe. She hadn't called her boys. She'd expected a phone. There could have been an accident and she wouldn't know. She pictured them crying, their arms reaching, and she wished she'd thought about it earlier and walked back over to the truck stop to call from a pay booth.

She thought of the girl at the desk and wondered if in boredom and cruelty she'd give a duplicate key and Louise's room number to a late-night guest and pretend it was a mistake when Louise screamed.

Later, she startled out of sleep reaching for a telephone ringing in her dreams.

The next day Louise called M. from a gas station in Blythe. "It's not a good day," he said. "Dinner with the producers." She didn't say anything. It was hard to talk to him when he was in the office. People were always there, listening, and he was guarded or brusque or spoke in a kind of code. If he said lunch — "We could have lunch or something" — it might be a euphemism, he might mean they could have the afternoon together and she should book a room, but she wouldn't know unless she asked, feeling for his meaning like in twenty questions. Finally he said, "I'll meet you after, but I'll only have a moment." He sounded impatient.

A little further along Louise pulled off the highway again and walked up among the Joshua trees and rock chimneys. It was finally warm under a postcard sky. In some ways the best time for her was beforehand, the anticipation. Time together was so brief she started bracing for his departure while he was still with her. For the moment everything seemed right with the world, certainty working like a drug in her veins.

She came in past Palm Desert from the east on I-10 and dropped down into San Bernardino in a blanket of smog. If you no longer lived there, did not have to worry about your lungs, fight the traffic, comprehend its vastness, Los Angeles had an appeal. Something narcotic in the atmosphere, dreams condensed in the amalgam of fumes.

She flowed into downtown, onto the Harbor, spilled out onto the Santa Monica, and crossed town to the 405 where she turned north again to Sunset, then west to Moira's. At Vicente Foods in Brentwood where a line of coral trees on the boulevard began a march to the sea, she stopped for flowers and champagne, tributes to the diva.

Moira came out the door as Louise pulled into the driveway, her mules slapping the bricks. "Hi, *darling!* How *are* you?" A voice gravelly from abuse, trained to project, always in italics. "Look at that *car!* Oh, *sweetie*, you're so *good!*" when she saw the delphiniums. A hug, pitched forward from the hips, kiss, kiss, then for a moment she drifted off, focused somewhere behind Louise. You lost her like that sometimes, and if you turned around to see what it was, there wouldn't be anything, only her own reflection in the car window capturing her attention. Then she was back, hooking arms. "Sweetheart! Come *in*."

Even in daylight Moira's living room was dark, an upholstered cavern, acoustically deadened by carpet and velvet and skirts on the tables.

"Shall we open it?" holding the champagne.

"Of course. Absolutely. But I've got to shower."

"No! You're not going out?"

"Later, I am. Just for coffee."

"But you've only just got here! Are you coming back?" Devastated.

Louise smiled. "Yes, I'm coming back. It's only for coffee."

One of Moira's looks. "So you say!" Then they were laughing, bumping against each other. "You're so bad," Moira said. She knew — knew something — how could she not? The calls and suspense, Louise's moods. But sworn to secrecy. And no name attached to the phantom lover.

Later they popped the champagne and Moira sat on the bed while Louise dressed. "Look how thin you are," Moira said. "Does he absolutely adore you?"

"He likes me, that's all."

"Oh, come *on*." Moira was married, but not particularly happy.

"It's true."

"How do you *do* it?"

"Do what? I like it like this. I know where I stand and he tells me no lies."

"*I'd* want to be adored."

"And you would be, too," said Louise.

Moira wanted to lend her something glamorous, pull her hair into a topknot, do her face. "Just a little color." Laughing, coming at her with a lipstick. But Louise wouldn't let her.

Louise's mother had never had a friend. She'd wrapped herself up in solitude like a winding sheet to keep herself intact. Louise was different, diminished, maybe, giving away her character along with her secrets. But she edited her confidences, shaded the truth with innuendo, creating a version of herself for Moira to embrace like an evolving rumor in which veracity was finally lost. Intimacy, like water or glass, distorted reality. Louise beguiled Moira, or maybe not. Maybe they played the same game, like paper dolls, allowing each other whatever guise they chose at the moment.

Sunset all the way to the Strip, the Towncar stately in the right lane, Beemers whining past on the banked curves. The champagne might have been a mistake.

Always the first moment she saw him, the confusion of adjusting her imagination to fit his reality. In her mind she had cut him down to size, made it manageable. Other people might not give a second glance, an ordinary man reading at a table in the restaurant below his office, but to her, she fell at his feet.

"So? How is it going?" His voice, the precision and lilt.

She sat down opposite him. "Fine. I'm fine. How about you?" Smiling, calm, trying to quiet the tumult inside.

"Yes, well, you know, trying to get an R instead of the X." He looked at her. He was tired, she could see it in his face. "You Americans. They make you go back and back."

"Is it sex? Or violence?"

"Violence, clearly. There is not very much sex." A smile, a look, then his thoughts went elsewhere as he drew patterns in spilled sugar with the handle of his spoon. He'd had a cappuccino while he waited. He looked up. "Do you want something?"

"I don't care."

"Come on, then. I'll show you."

Maybe he'd accomplished so much in his life because he moved quickly. She trailed him, the tail of the comet. Out of the restaurant, into the lobby, past the guard. A kiss in the elevator a warmer hello. His floor — quiet, dim. A confusing maze of corridors and cubicles. If he left her she'd never find her way out, but familiar to him as home. During the days there'd be dozens of people, greetings as he walked the halls, questions, decisions to be made, pressures and anxieties, office intrigues, battles and jealousies, crushes and love affairs, gossip, everyone attached somehow to him. She envied his place in the world and the people who populated this floor and had a legitimate claim on him.

Voices somewhere down a hall, someone working late. He took her hand and drew her into the editing room, closing the door and locking it behind them. He smiled in the dark. A commando who had attained his objective. Neon from Sunset striped the walls and a river of headlights wheeled across the ceiling. He kissed her.

In the dark her confidence returned. She wanted him compromised, wanted him to go further than he intended, wanted him out there on the very edge where she was.

They were quick and quiet, only their breath. She'd leave her ghost in the editing room like a flag on Everest. Tomorrow when he came in he'd cut his eyes to the couch, remembering.

Afterwards, he ran a reel on the editing table for her, slow-motion mayhem. He showed her where he would cut and use another angle, snip out the image of a blade going in, blood spurting, try to get it past the board. Degrees of gore too fine to calibrate, solemnly adjudicated.

He thought it was the war causing his fascination with violence, growing up amid bombs and rubble, danger every-where, more alive then than at any time since. Louise thought it was his mother loving him so absolutely that he integrated with his dark side, never developed a censor.

When she asked he showed her Lina, an apparent nonentity in a crowded shot, but Louise knew better. He would have memorized every frame and his eye would fly immediately to her.

They left without being seen. He let her off in the lobby, kissed her quickly. "I'll call you," he said, then continued

95

down to parking. She walked out alone, up Sunset to where she'd left the car. Nobody's baby. He left her no illusions.

There was too much time. A few appointments straddling the weekend, keeping her in town. She was marooned, waiting, and she wanted to be back on the road. She was smoking and had given up trying not to, promising herself she would stop again at home. She tried to work in longhand, sitting beside the pool at Moira's house, a glass of wine for elevenses, but she couldn't concentrate. Couldn't think in longhand anymore, needed her computer.

She telephoned everyone she knew, left messages all over town, and was immediately sorry. At Moira's the phone rang constantly and no one ever answered. Four rings, then a long silence while the message played, giving her time to make it to the kitchen from wherever she was to hear the caller's voice. But she seldom picked up, even when it was for her. She hardly left the house, afraid to go out. Afraid M. would call and she'd miss it and they'd forget to tell her, or pretend to forget to tell her. He *would* call, he'd said he would, but she knew never to ask when. She was like a specimen, a rat in a Skinner box conditioned by torment and reward, training herself to wait. And at the same time outside of herself, observing the experiment, the mounting anxiety.

At the last minute she agreed to meet Iris at a party, someone's anniversary. There was valet parking right on Beverly Glen where it was dangerous to even slow down, and a shuttle bus up the side of the canyon to the house. Louise was afraid someone would clip the Lincoln roaring around a corner. Living here you could never keep a cat.

Up at the house the wind soughed in pines around the pool and the traffic below sounded like a river. There was hardly anyone she knew. She was underdressed. Afternoon, she'd thought, and Iris said casual. There was wine, but no one else was drinking. Everyone looked dazed or worried as though there'd been bad news, some sort of apocalyptic announcement just before she arrived. An AA anniversary, she realized belatedly, the effort of abstention, the eternal vigilance, life measured out in units of sobriety, every day or week or year a cause célèbre, but no way to put teeth into the festivity. Suck down another cranberry seltzer.

Behind her someone was talking about M., a man's voice. "He wants changes. Sixty percent of the script. Or more. Can you believe it? He's very confrontational." She turned around and looked. A writer from her old agency, making a big splash now with a picture nominated. He mouthed hello but she knew he couldn't place her.

Someone else said, "People I know say he's crazy. Talented, but impossible. You wouldn't want to work with him." Louise walked away. She didn't want to hear. M. had told her about the project, a period epic that would take him back to Mexico. She hoped he wouldn't do it.

She gave Moira's number to a director just out from New York who walked her down the hill holding her elbow, afraid she'd stumble, and fussed about her driving home. The sanctimony of the reformed. She'd only had a little wine. She supposed she should be touched by his concern and pleased he wanted to see her. She couldn't think of any reason to tell him no.

The next day he picked her up and drove her out to the ocean. They parked on the Palisades and took stairs down to a caged footbridge across the Pacific Coast Highway. The dismal smell of urine, an empty six-pack, a used rubber. She imagined kids doing it there as a feat of some sort, suspended over the traffic, defying an earthquake. He was holding her hand.

97

It was warm in town, but a cold wind blew off the water. She could find nothing to say. She hated his white toes when he took off his cowboy boots, like something you'd find under a rock. She went somewhere else, closed a door, while he kissed her. Enduring a medical procedure. His breath was stale and his tongue cool, a fish darting in her mouth. All she wanted was to go home.

"I'm sorry," she said. "It isn't you." He moved her hair off her face and tilted her chin to look in her eyes. He wanted someone, he was on the wagon, ready. A new leaf. He'd be good to her, patient and earnest. It was her divorce, she told him. She needed more time. Lying, but she couldn't say it's another man, it's my married man.

Back at Moira's no one was home and no messages were written down on the pad by the phone. She swallowed half a valium and washed the sand out of her hair. Hours later, long after M. would have left the office, Moira's husband remembered to tell her that someone had called for her that morning, a foreign gentleman, as he archly put it, while he was on the other line long distance. "Sorry, I forgot to tell you." He gave her a searching look, pretending to be perplexed by her distress. The games they played.

How many times, Louise wondered, had she stayed in this hotel? Low-ceilinged pastel suites where mirrors multiplied space. They knew her at the desk. Everything was familiar. The silver matches that left metallic flecks like glitter on her fingers, the fragrance of the lotion, the ring of the phone, so soft it was almost inaudible when he called from the lobby or from his office to say he was on his way. This was the last time.

"Maybe we should stop," M. had said. He put on a solemn face like a doctor delivering bad news. She wanted to hit him.

"Why?"

"It's the lying. You know, thinking of something to say. Why I'm late, why I'm leaving the office." She wondered what had happened. Some inquisition, his wife or a producer. Some small shift in the balance between cost and desire.

He told her at dinner. Easy, she thought, to tell her then, afterwards, as though he'd thought, "One last time and then I'll tell her." He should have told her beforehand. She would like to have known, made it a requiem fuck. Or not done it. If she'd known, maybe she'd have chosen not to. He should have told her at the hotel at least, risked tears and mopping up. Now there was nothing she could say.

After dinner he walked her up the street to Tower to select music for the Lincoln. "What do you want?" he asked. "What do you like?"

"I don't care," she said. "You choose." He bought her Mahler and Handel. Water music and songs of the earth. She felt like a child — a treat for behaving herself at the dentist's. She imagined throwing a tantrum instead, which was what she felt like doing, refusing the bribe, sobbing, screaming at him, flinging herself out into the traffic, catapulted from fender to fender like a hockey puck, a tabloid sensation. But she wanted the music and she let him buy it for her, something from him to keep after he was gone. He'd never given her anything before, no silk or silver or leather bound notebooks. Richard had showered her with gifts.

M. asked if she'd go back to Moira's or stay all night in the room. He thought it was dreary for her alone in the hotel, but she preferred the solitude and the continuing connection to him and she was embarrassed to check out without staying. So when the phone murmured her heart leapt. A reprieve. He'd changed his mind and was calling to take it back.

But it was her father. Moira had given him the number. Louise thought that after what she had seen she shouldn't have been surprised, but she wasn't prepared for the finality. Grandma was dead.

The next morning Louise bought a black dress and a ticket back to Texas and left the Lincoln at a park-and-fly lot out near the airport.

ten

THEY CONVENED IN San Antonio. A tall elderly physician addressed respectfully here as Doctor. Pale, somber, burdened always by his responsibilities and reflections, imposing in a fedora, which, in old affectation, now habit, he angled sharply over one eye. The requisite doffings lent him a courtly, attentive manner. Three grown children, Leland, Louise and Anne, unmistakably his, fond and deferential. And Julia, elegant always, the Viennese, her cap of snowy hair reaching barely to his shoulder, Anne's mother, so long the second wife it seemed there had never been another.

He had booked them into the Fairmount, an old stone hotel a few blocks south of the Alamo, renovated to a kind of Lone Star grandeur. They flew in on Friday night at different times from different corners of the continent. The children shared a suite, like someone else's family or a Marx brothers routine, adults at a slumber party, politely deferring use of the bathroom to each other. The hotel staff must have wondered what brought them together and what their relationships were to one another.

In the morning, before the burial, they assembled in the dining room. It was a peculiar family, Louise thought, self declared gentry, observing a strict standard of rectitude. So quiet at their table they could hear each other swallow, the pop of a mandibular joint, the clink of a knife. Composure modulated character into impenetrability, objectivity eclipsed personality. So little was given away from behind the fortress of decorum you wondered if anyone was at home. She had to watch herself, keep a lid on.

The hearse met them at the cemetery. The mortician had left Midland at three in the morning with Grandma in the back.

Louise imagined his long drive east into an accelerated dawn. She wondered if his wife had gotten up with him in darkness and fixed him a thermos of coffee, what they'd talked about and what he'd listened to on the radio, if there was a radio in the hearse. Talk radio for company instead of a dirge.

Her heels sank into the earth as they walked toward the grave. She tip-toed, coming last, bringing up the rear, as always a Uranus in distant orbit. She wished she'd brought flowers, a big sheaf of iris, a nod to convention, a visible tribute. She was glad she'd been the last of them to see Grandma alive, as though that claim could stitch her into place in the family.

A carpet of Astroturf was laid over the cured brown grass, a canvas awning erected above folding chairs set out in rows in anticipation of a congregation whose absence was thus made manifest. A pink coffin rested above the grave — Louise wondered who had chosen *that* — the upper half of the lid lifted.

They gathered in a loose semi-circle and Louise gazed down upon a stranger's face. Her father must have felt the same, for after a moment he said, "Well. This face displays more serenity than it did in life." There was something of Grandma there, to be sure, the nose was hers and the jutting brows, the soft Gibson girl pompadour that hadn't changed her entire life, except to turn to white. Her knobby old hands wound up her thin rope of hair, inserting combs and pins by feel, too modest for a mirror. Slow as molasses her whole life, like something cold-blooded, a tortoise, blinking slowly, turning her head with great deliberation. Son, she called Louise's father, stretching out the sound, her drawl adding syllables. She might be saying sun, center of my universe.

Louise preferred to remember her as she'd seen her in Midland, her face collapsed and distorted. The serenity was suspect, foreign, something injected under her skin to smooth the wrinkles, her lips and eyes sewn shut with an invisible trade stitch. Pretty, but alien, like someone made over at a department store cosmetics counter. It wasn't Grandma, but it was enough to evoke her.

Julia read a eulogy for a mother-in-law she had despised. Anne cried. Louise's father recited prepared remarks, eloquent but impersonal, politely synopsizing his mother's life as though there might be strangers listening, leaving out the scorn and pity she had actually elicited in him. Louise wanted somehow to say she was glad for her Southern roots, but couldn't find the words. Or she wished she could muster the bravura to render a cappella "We Shall Gather" or "Abide With Me" — Grandma would have liked a hymn — but she couldn't.

And then they gazed in silence at a woman who had long outlived their love.

They were expected to walk away from the mechanics of interment. It caused consternation that Louise's father wanted to wait. The workers who might have laughed and talked, maybe slipped a beer from a cooler in the back of someone's pickup, now had to accomplish all the prosaic tasks associated with burial under the mourners' gaze with an appropriate solemnity.

The Astroturf was removed and folded and rolled with ceremony fit for a flag. The coffin was lowered into a concrete sarcophagus, necessary, they were told, to prevent sinking caused by drainage problems. A forklift had to place a cement lid over the coffin before the grave was filled, but the structure of the awning interfered. The chairs were folded up and stacked, more Astroturf rolled, the pipes uncoupled and the tent dismantled. The mortician directed all of these proceedings like an inept stage manager caught in the footlights as the curtain went up, unexpectedly having to preside in front of an audience.

The earth removed from the grave had vanished. They didn't want you to see dirt and think of worms. Finally it arrived in a trailer pulled behind a tractor. Flat headstones were moved out of the way to allow the tractor to back the trailer into position to dump the earth, conjuring in Louise's mind the prank of scrambling markers, causing flowers to be placed above strangers' bones. Something kids might get up to at Halloween. She hadn't known they were simply laid down, impermanent as flagstones, weight and respect alone holding them in place.

Louise's father wanted a shovel. A tool of the trade, you would have thought, but someone had to be sent in search of one. Then they each scattered a ritual spade-full of dirt — a bleak rain of pebbles — and finally it was over.

At the curb the mortician shook Louise's father's hand and asked, perplexed, "What kind of doctor are you?" Louise laughed. There was something clerical about her father, to be sure — his solemn demeanor, his carefully chosen words. He could have been a doctor of divinity, doyen of some peculiar sect, but if he were his following was only them.

They walked then on cobblestone paths inside the perimeter of the huge stockade at the Mission of San Jose. Grandma's long span of history and the ceremony they'd just completed connected Louise to past events. This mission had stood once under siege on an open plain, stormed by riled tribes, and now they walked in Saturday peace while outside the walls a city sprawled. Two of Grandma's lifetimes end to end would take them back to that day, and all the living and dying from then to now differed only in particulars.

As long as they were in San Antonio Julia wanted to see the sights, the Alamo, the line in the sand, Bowie's knife, and whatever else. Later they walked on the Paseo del Rio, lunched in sunshine beside the river. The family watched askance as Louise shook Tabasco onto her omelette, squeezed lime into her beer, then afterwards walked away to sit alone and smoke, excessive and peculiar, a cuckoo in the finch's nest, her lineage in question. She didn't belong to this family, was only marginally part of it. She was her mother's, had remained her mother's, a fierce, loyal buttress during the agonizing summers when Julia did her over at Macy's and the hairdresser's, aghast at the homemade dresses, grayed cotton underpants, and impossible sewing-scissors coiffures. She scrubbed dirt from Louise's neck with alcohol and paraded her at dinner in tasteful new frocks. Leland was wooed away. He left Louise and her mother and his dog Smoky, his seventh-grade friends and one hundred Rhode Island reds, a never-to-be-completed boy scout project, and moved permanently out to San Francisco where he went to the best of schools and had a room of his own, a microscope, walrus tusk chess set and a perfect little sister in a blue dress. But at the end of every visit Louise flew home to the secure, subversive certainty of her mother's depression and poverty and neglect.

In the afternoon they walked into an emptied and decrepit downtown that Louise thought made her father mournful. Anne was looking for the pecan pralines that Grandma used to send. Louise could have told her they were from Lamme's in Austin, not from San Antonio at all. Among the children she was the only Texan and she had the longest memory.

At a shoeshine stand a Mexican man hammered new heels onto Louise's impractical pumps while she stood on one foot, then the other, and the family waited. They'd walked that far.

Louise's father couldn't remember the number of the old house, or the cross street, wasn't certain how to reach the neighborhood, and didn't seem eager for the expedition. But as they got closer he found shops and intersections and railroad crossings familiar. Louise thought it was like breaking into a sealed room and finding intact a whole forgotten history that had been there all along, preserved behind a closed door.

Her father had remade himself when he left Texas. He'd dropped his colloquialisms, taught himself to speak all over again in what he called stage English, carefully unaccented diction so that to meet him no one would discern a Southern boyhood. He had abandoned himself, never integrated his past with the man he made of himself, his own creation. Louise was now his last Southern vestige. No wonder she tried him.

He looked pained and anxious gazing out the car window — insecure, as though betrayed by his imperfect recollection, an intellectual man assailed by emotion. He frowned as though straining to hear a conversation carried on in another room, and squinted through the tunnel of time. Several times he said, "There, that's it," then took it back. "No, I guess not, after all." But they found it. As soon as he saw the address he remembered, though the house had changed, the veranda gone, and neighboring houses stood where once there'd been vacant lots. They got out of the car and stared.

The surrounding houses needed paint and repairs, the yards were bare, choked with last season's weeds or worn to dirt by dogs. Pickups were parked in the driveways and dogs barked at the ends of their chains. An ominous bass throbbed from a car traveling nearby. Louise imagined the spectacle of privilege her family made standing in the street all dressed in black. Julia wanted to go, afraid the residents would set upon them, but Louise felt at home. In every instance, she thought, she was bonded with some nether side — the functionaries, the

Hispanics, the displaced — and only accidentally attached to her family.

She watched her father. The family shared that present moment, saw the same house and tangle of bare branches overhead, the same dusk sky closed down upon them all, and they would recall it similarly, except for him. No empathic leap could bridge the gulf of experience. With the passage of his mother there was no one left to share his history. Louise was sorry she couldn't know him better, not as he was, but as he'd once been, someone she might have preferred.

That night in the hotel dining room they celebrated the convocation of family with champagne. No spouses or children to fracture nuclear allegiance. Louise wondered what the hotel staff thought now. Revelers in mourning.

eleven

THREE HOPS FROM San Antonio back to Los Angeles, an aerial replay of the route she'd driven. She could trace the highways she'd traveled below. They put down in El Paso and again in Phoenix where Louise left her father and Julia, changed planes, and was alone again, relieved of the effort of sociability.

It was late when she got in. They'd buried the Lincoln at the Budget lot, parked it back against the fence behind a sea of cars, with only a single open slot to maneuver in and out of. Liberating it was like working one of those children's puzzles in which letters slide around in a plastic frame to form the alphabet. Finally reunited, she slid the Mahler into the tape player and drove home to Moira's.

In Mexico when M. had left her alone in her room Louise had stood in the window and smoked her cigarette and calculated. The whole world was sleeping. She imagined the ring of the telephone in a distant house, Moira's, say, and the shock of fear as she fumbled to answer, adrenaline startling her into wakefulness. What would she say, though? It wasn't an hour when you could call a friend simply to hear a familiar voice. But the hotel switchboard never slept, nor the airline reservations clerks. Theirs were voices that would answer in the night, accommodate her wishes, and calm her with their normalcy.

Louise knew what she should do. It would be best to leave. Best for him, but for her as well. Preserve her dignity, retire gracefully. In the morning, finding her gone, he might be pricked with regret. She could imagine he would be, though she'd never know. He wouldn't pursue her, ask her to stay or to return. It was what she ought to do, but she couldn't bear to, could not bear for that to have been the last of him.

It gave her something to do, and her own voice attempting Spanish in salutation rooted her again in existence. She speaks, therefore she is. They answer, therefore she is not alone. Her machinations were clever. She didn't book the first flight out, but she took a seat on the afternoon plane. He'd never dream she lied when she said the morning flight was full, he'd never think of checking and never guess her regret was feigned.

So, in the morning she called his room as though nothing lay between them, as though the inconvenience of Lina was only that, as though her heart wasn't broken, as though it was nothing much to her one way or the other. "I thought it'd be best if I left a little early," she said. "You know, perhaps it'd be easier for you, too. I've changed my reservation, but the first flight I could get leaves this afternoon. Shall we have a cup of coffee before I go?"

Clever girl. She disarmed him. She could hear it in his voice. He was touched by her acceptance, moved by her grace. She was independent and dignified, after all, required nothing of him, and coffee would be pleasant. It had worked. She'd teetered but was still on the wire.

They met in the lobby. To look at her you wouldn't know. A calm woman in a T-shirt and a narrow skirt. No sign of tears, no look of cunning. They went out into the sunlight and walked, an apparent couple, like tourists, distancing themselves from possible recognition.

She let him talk about Lina. Listening worked like glue, cementing him to her, and his account threw water on the witch in her imagination. Over coffee Lina dissolved into nothing more than a Rorschach that reflected M.'s own longing for reunion with something vanished in himself. A little muchacha he couldn't even talk to. Only an idea, something he dreamed up and fastened onto.

Louise had checked out, left her bag with the concierge, but after coffee, when there was still an hour before she had to leave, M. took her to his suite. The disarray of his rooms opened her eyes to the cherished boy, beloved of his mother, and for the moment he was divested of his magic and she looked tenderly on him, an indulged prince she allowed to imperiously command her. It made her smile, a tyrant in the nursery.

The following morning, back from San Antonio, she telephoned M. It gave her the shakes. She was afraid he wouldn't take the call and didn't know what she'd do. But he came on the line. Easier than she'd dared hope, nothing to it.

"I've been to Texas," she said, "and back again since we last spoke. Now I'm leaving, heading home."

"When?"

"In the morning."

"Oh," he said, sounding breezy. "Shall we have something then, before you go? Some coffee or something?"

"Sure," she said. "If you'd like." A reprieve, like in Mexico. All she'd hoped for and she didn't even have to ask. She'd braced herself for nothing. But she wouldn't try to make anything of it. She'd see him. It was enough.

In Brentwood at Moira's, lying on the bed in the guest room with the windows opened onto the camellias, reading in the dim green light, Spanish was all Louise heard. Nannies called to each other or to children in staccato bursts, gardeners shouted over the racket of their mowers and blowers. It was, in its way, as foreign as Mexico. Here all the tasks that gave Louise's life shape and meaning were consigned while the señoras lunched and had their legs waxed, visited their shrinks or played tennis. Less affluent neighborhoods were deserted and silent during the days, but here a cheering sense of population prevailed. Help lived in or drove up from South Central in pickups or big battered relics from before the oil embargo. The manicured street took on a village atmosphere. Moira's housekeeper knew the gardeners, nannies, and pool men up and down the block. Their chatter and racket was comforting even though Louise was remote from it. Moira was out.

Louise couldn't concentrate enough to read. She was at sea on a damask counterpane inside a brass four-poster. Without work or chores and obligations time had no meaning and the day became featureless, passed imperceptibly.

She pulled on her bathing suit and went out to the pool, sliding into water warm as a bath. Once, after partying all night, she swam naked at dawn with Moira, her husband, and an English playwright who waded in wearing his tuxedo and lapped the pool in a stately breast stroke, holding his head up out of the water. Moira attracted such people, or inspired such behavior, Louise wasn't sure which. Buoyant and sleek in her skin, illuminated from below, Louise had sliced through the water like a dolphin, cutting capers around the playwright while Moira sat laughing on the steps in the shallow end.

Now bottle brush shed scarlet threads onto the surface of the turquoise water and an automatic cleaner chugged softly about, vacuuming the pool as though animated by appetite or intelligence. Louise did a leisurely side stroke up and back that hardly disturbed the water.

It was January, but you wouldn't know it. Here the leaves stayed on the trees, and year round day and night remained equally divided. At home in Seattle the sun, if it shone at all, barely cleared the horizon, but at the summer solstice sunshine poured through the northern windows long into the evenings. You knew the season by the angle of the light. As you approached the equator time and seasons lost delineation. You had to think to remember the month. And in Los Angeles, if you had the liberty, you adjusted your day to avoid traffic. Office hours became eleven to seven, lunch at three, dinner at nine. Louise felt suspended in time and space as she swam, as though the elements of air and water had blended and gravity dissolved.

This part of the sojourn was at its end. Tomorrow, after coffee, she'd head north through Victorville and Barstow, Las Vegas, and on to Salt Lake and Park City where the film festival was in progress. The thrust of the Lincoln piercing the wind like fabric ripping, a long gash north, hundreds of miles of Nevada and Utah rolling silently under her wheels while Mahler's songs of despair blasted.

But departures were difficult. Until she was actually underway she was loathe to go. Now she didn't want to return, wanted to stay in the sanctuary of Moira's green guest room. Without the pressure of a scheduled departure, a flight to catch, it was hard to choose the moment to go.

In the morning Louise glided up the bricked alley to the entrance of the Bel Age, allowed the valet to hand her out, and the doorman to usher her in as though the marble and polished brass, fountains, mirrors and art were her domain. She was instructed by her possession of the Lincoln in exactly the way she supposed her father had intended. If you thought well of yourself, it appeared, treated yourself to luxury, the world accepted your view of yourself and accorded you value. In exchange for that enhanced perception you looked more benignly back out upon the world.

They'd met here before. She liked seeing him first thing in the morning, fresh from the shower, his hair still wet and combed neatly back. Later, it would stick out and up and fall across his forehead. He was without vanity. Seemed without vanity. Louise could not imagine him selecting a shirt. Maybe while he swam laps his wife laid out his day's clothes so he wouldn't have to choose. He was fresh from his swim, the shower, from his wife, and the mysteries of his home. She wondered if he kissed her as he left, kissed his girls, breezing out without coffee, saying, "I've got a breakfast meeting, see you tonight." Though not those words precisely because at home they wouldn't speak in English. Then whipping down Beverly Glen. It surprised her that with so much on his mind he even remembered; he never wrote it down.

He asked for a four-minute egg, balancing it in the mouth of a tiny jam jar when it came in a bowl instead of a cup. Only one way to eat a boiled egg. It reminded her of childhood and of her mother, of toast fingers and bed trays. She thought of his childhood, the bounty of a war-time egg, the hens long since gone to the pot.

He was as always, as though nothing had changed. Pleasant and conversational. He was reading scripts, he said, searching for possibilities that interested him. Strange things appealed, weird extremes, evangelicals and bugs from space. There was so much he could get his mind around, a reach that dazzled her. The epic in Mexico was now unlikely. They'd run a budget, he said, and it was too expensive.

"Too bad," she said, smiling, ironic.

"Not at all. It's so unpleasant. Everyone gets sick and there's nothing to do but fall in love." Meaning Lina, teasing her.

The time of day and the meal seemed innocent and ordinary, domestic, really. She might be his wife. She arrested time, held it in abeyance, and for an hour refused the future.

As they left, walking through the lobby, he smiled at her and linked arms and snugged her against his side. "It's not so bad, is it?" he asked, "Just to chat?" He did know, then. He remembered, he hadn't forgotten that he'd said it was over. But mentally she leapt with jubilance, the victor after a close match, her fist in the air, certain she'd won continuation, that they'd go on as before. She'd be back.

"No, not so bad," she said.

Even so, she dreaded her car arriving — or worse, his coming first — and the moment of parting. The air was soft and cool. Louise thought she could smell the sea in the haze. Soon the sun would burn it off, but by then she'd be gone. She wouldn't know what kind of a day it turned into, or what it held for him. At that moment Los Angeles seemed like a safe haven, the only place on earth she wanted to be. That moment, standing beside him under the porte-cochere, was all there was of life, the moment before ascending to the block, a last treasured instant.

The car came, her Lincoln gliding to a stop, then the small rushed flurry of good-bye as other cars stacked up behind it and the valet waited beside the opened door while M. kissed her and held her briefly against him, then released her, and she had to go.

She slid in, the door closed. She flung a last glance over her shoulder at him as she pulled away. He waved. When she checked the rearview mirror at the bottom of the drive he was no longer looking after her.

twelve

ONCE, BRIEFLY, IN another lifetime it seemed, Louise had lived in Las Vegas while Richard was producing a crime series there. He put her up at the Golden Nugget in a two-story suite that looked down on Fremont Avenue, a neon canyon lit amber by thousands of bulbs in Binion's Golden Horseshoe. Mirrored ceilings, black leather and gilt, sybaritic plumbing — a Jacuzzi with a view of the street, steam jets in the shower. One of a whole wing of luxury suites so anyone who wished could feel like a high roller, impress his girl.

Now she pulled off the freeway as a test, a challenge to dormant demons. She thought she might resurrect something, some old anguish or residual longing. She parked and walked inside out of the heat and glare into the perpetual nocturnal glamour of the casino. Low ceilings and plush carpeting muted the electronic din of the slot machines — wired sound effects, cascading synthetic notes that might be supposed to suggest tumbling coins. Not so long ago the noise would have been mechanical, the sound of gears and levers, metal striking metal as your dollar dropped.

The demons were inert. The remembered misery was no longer attached to the man who caused it, or even to the irony of the anachronistic conjunction of Las Vegas and divorce, but clung to an image of a woman she'd never really been, someone from an earlier decade, a snapshot in someone else's family album, a disgraced aunt or a cousin who had vanished or died young whose story no one clearly recalled, a face in a photograph behind whose captured smile a whole history was lost.

Sometimes in the afternoons she had gone out to the 7-Eleven for cigarettes, her purse weighted with quarters, and played the poker machines there beside plate glass windows smoked against the sun, killing the hours. Or inexplicably wandered grocery store aisles and bought food she never cooked, couldn't cook in the suite, lamb chops and pasta and salad greens, which spoiled in the tiny refrigerator under the bar.

Once she had driven Richard's rented car out into the desert hoping to find a dirt road into the hills where she could walk, but instead became lost in a wasteland of gullies filled with refuse. Shelves of rock scraped the oil pan and she imagined herself high-centered in a canyon of old bedsprings and used Pampers, stuck and having to walk for help. She thought that if she looked she might discover a body, an arm sticking up out of a hastily dug grave, a hit victim, or somebody's baby, carrion disturbed by crows or coyotes.

In the bar one night she ordered a lethal succession of outmoded cocktails — pink ladies, cuba libres, and manhattans in memory of her mother. In the middle of the night she went up to the suite and sat in the Jacuzzi until she wrinkled like a raisin, watching them shoot a car chase over and over in the street below. A fire truck hosed the pavement for the effect of rain, then a Chrysler with fins like sharks' dorsals careened through the throng of equipment and fish-tailed around the corner.

She could pick Richard out of the crowd. Amber light on a golden mane. He carried a phone in his jacket pocket and she dialed the number. "Look up," she said when he answered, and stepped onto the edge of the tub, plastering herself against the glass, arms and legs akimbo like a suction cup doll stuck to the inside of a car window. Other eyes followed his, an audience for her antics. He turned away and when she climbed back down he had turned off his phone.

Her images of those times were bleached as though overexposed to neon or sunlight, thin, like bad negatives that wouldn't print. She imagined herself brittle, a glass figurine charged in harmonic response to some distant unseen nuclear detonation.

She had lost track of herself, her soul had escaped, and now she was back like an aimless spirit haunting old precincts in search of she didn't know what. Innocence, perhaps, or optimism that had vanished in her like a tail or a fourth molar, phased out from long disuse, a genetic mutation that would die out with her.

She bought a roll of quarters for old times' sake and sipped bourbon and water while she played the slots. Before getting back onto the interstate she drove the strip. In daylight the neon had a quixotic valor.

The sun hung low behind her, threw long shadows across the bench, and lit the Wasatch Range mauve and gold under an incoming front. At Nephi, when she stopped for gas the first little skiff of snow was chasing around the pumps. Louise thought she could make Salt Lake, only sixty miles north, but she didn't calculate on the combined velocity of the Lincoln and the storm. By Spanish Fork there were six inches on the road and the snow was falling so heavily into her headlights that she couldn't see the shoulder or the brake lights ahead of her. She passed lines of chain reaction collisions, crawling fearfully past in a carnival of colored strobes pulsing from the roofs of police cars and tow trucks, warnings diffused by the falling snow so they gave no sense of depth or distance.

Snow packed and froze on the windshield, the wipers slapped clear an ever diminishing oval of glass. Louise was tired and longed to stop, but she thought it was more treacherous to pull over than to go on: someone might slam into her from behind. Finally a pink glow to the right suggested neon, the lure of an exit, and she angled cautiously off the interstate.

In the motel parking lot she fell, her feet going out from under her on a sheet of ice that lay beneath the snow. She went down hard on her hip and elbow. She struggled quickly back to her feet as another car pulled into the lot, pinning her in its lights. Stand straight, don't limp, avoid eye contact, perhaps her composure would make him question his senses, think the image of her fall was an illusion created by swirled snow. She had felt like a beetle on its back, vulnerable and ridiculous. But now, upright again, holding onto the fender for support, afraid to trust her footing, she wished for a compassionate arm to encircle her, for sympathy to unleash tears. She slung a look from the sides of her eyes, but the driver of the other car honored her now-defunct wish for privacy. He saw that she was up and looked away.

One kind word and she'd cry. Cry in fatigue, in relief to be off the road with a bed at hand, and for her helplessness as she fell on the ice; but more, she'd cry in momentary suspension of her vigilance against despair and self-pity. She longed now to weep in a stranger's arms, to surrender to a Samaritan's kindness. He'd been portly, she'd seen, in a tan windbreaker and wire glasses. Someone's husband, a father, she supposed, a salesman, pharmaceuticals or aluminum siding, within reach of home, but detained by the weather. She'd avoided a chance encounter that perhaps they'd both have remembered.

She might have asked him in to share her bourbon after he'd escorted her across the ice, exchanged with him the sketch of a life, bestowed upon him the valor of a savior, and let him go amplified by his benevolence. She would have given him the chair and she'd perch on the edge of the bed, still in her anorak while the wall heater labored. They'd touch toothbrush glasses and talk about the storm, where it caught them and where they were headed. He'd gallantly retire after one drink when the chill was off the room. Later, he might jack off in the shower and wonder at himself that he'd let an opportunity pass. In the morning he'd watch her scrape her windshield from behind his curtain. They would never see each other again, but the encounter would remain permanently preserved for each of them like a fly in amber.

Instead, she crossed the parking lot alone in a cautious shuffle. He glanced her way as he unlocked his door, a small impersonal inquiry, but she looked quickly away, afraid she'd telegraph some sort of invitation.

Louise called her answering machine. Richard, whom she had thought she loved, her Las Vegas boyfriend, the hibiscus man who had ended her marriage, had broken a year's silence. His recorded voice speaking into her ear was so familiar that at first she didn't feel shock, but when she hung up her hands were trembling. "Jesus Christ," she breathed. "Jesus." She was drinking the bourbon alone, without the companionship of the unknown Samaritan, and was light-headed already. Outside the storm continued unabated.

If she'd been at home she might not have called back, but alone in a motel it seemed like an anonymous experiment devoid of consequence, impermanent, like writing on slate that you could wipe away, or not attributable to her, as if she had become as generic as the room. Too, it was like a conjuring trick, as though the pilgrimage to Las Vegas had produced him, impossible not to see it as cause and effect, as if she had tapped into a vein of unsuspected power. Louise dialed his number from memory. "Hi," she said when he answered, and then, taking nothing for granted, "It's Louise."

"You only just caught me," he said. "I'm leaving in the morning for Salt Lake." A confluence that would once have seemed designed by divine ordinance now seemed comic in its mis-timing She felt the power of indifference.

"How funny," she said. "Guess where I'm calling from."

The storm left deep snow in its wake, groomed now into packed powder, a bonanza for the resorts. The sky was brilliantly azure, cloudless, and it was warm enough to ski without gloves. Louise skied alone. She preferred to be alone, though Iris was somewhere on the slopes, cruising the runs and the lift lines for people she knew or wanted to know. The film festival was underway, an annual excursion among movie people to Park City for schussing and schmoozing.

Rare to be completely in the moment, Louise thought, focused, alert to sensation with no thought of past or future. Swimming was sometimes like that, and skiing. Her mind gave over its perpetual anxious wrangling and became simply the control panel of a guided missile, all its faculties intent on speed, bank, and approaching hazard, the survival instinct in every cell compelling her mass to cooperative performance. At the bottom and on the lift she marshalled her forces for another sally. She smoked on the ride up, enjoying the contradictory pleasure of a cigarette at high altitude where the crystal air was already thin and insufficient.

She exhausted herself. At the end of the day she felt dessicated like a sponge, squeezed flat by the compression of concentration. In need of a bath or the hot tub.

She had no idea how it was going to feel to see Richard again. She only remembered how it had used to be when he seemed incandescent to her, as though he radiated light or was tracked by a celestial spot. They were meeting for dinner. He'd researched the restaurants, sussed out what was chic. She dawdled getting ready, not worrying so much about her appearance but trying to ensure a margin of lateness. He'd keep you waiting, anyone at all, just to make certain that he could, and to make sure you knew he was busy, his calendar jammed. But when he arrived he'd be contrite, swearing he'd tried, he'd promised himself, for once in his life, on your account, but the best laid plans and yada, yada, yada.

She got there before him, even so. She ordered a drink and reflected on timeliness and manners while she waited. Punctuality impressed her more. M., for instance, was never late.

She watched his entrance, the stir he created at the hostess's podium, shifting his overflowing satchel and an armful of scripts to crane at the reservations book, then searching the room, seeing her, throwing up his hands, as much as he could, burdened as he was, and rolling toward her through the tables in his bomber jacket, smiling his rueful smile. She could have predicted every moment of it.

She smiled back, but it confused and saddened her. There was no perceptible tremor in her heart. She had believed she loved him, but now the feeling was so emphatically gone she had to question what it had been in the first place.

He greeted her with a presumptive warmth, then immediately disrupted her, standing there looking around with his arm in the air, summoning. They had to move, the table was wrong, not what he'd asked for. Something more intimate, back against the wall. Everything a production. The right chardonnay and something exquisite that wasn't on the menu, but the chef would know. Louise was annoyed and liberated. Two hours to get through, and very little to say.

Later, he got the Lincoln stuck in the snow at the bottom of the driveway of the cottage he was renting. He had a four-wheel drive from Avis, but in the afternoon he'd walked down the hill to the movies and so arrived at the restaurant on foot. After dinner he asked Louise for a lift home. Out of the habit of deference, no longer germane, she let him drive, and she could have told him he should stop at the top of the incline.

He rammed in and out of reverse, trying futilely to rock it, wrapping the engine senselessly while the tires screamed and spun. The car would have catapulted backwards if they'd suddenly found traction. He slammed the door when he got out, an infantile gesture. He'd get her a tow in the morning, he said, and proposed she stay the night. A Freudian spin suddenly illuminated the accident of bad judgment.

Louise was not even tempted. She felt flat and sad, weary of his company. He drove her back to her condominium in his rented Jeep in silence, furious with the Towncar and with her, witness to his blunder.

The next day it should have been a simple enough matter to collect the car and head for home, stay overnight in Boise and make Seattle the following day, but snow was falling again and Louise was afraid, thinking of the Lincoln in the snow, its wheels locking, skidding, its massive weight lending impetus, picking up speed like an unwieldy torpedo.

She got halfway down the hill to Salt Lake and pulled into a gas station to consult the weather service. All she could get was a recorded forecast. She wanted a human voice, someone down in Salt Lake who would look out a window and up at the sky, or a trucker who'd come in from Idaho over Sweetzer Summit, someone with some empirical evidence, someone who'd speculate, hazard a guess, advise her. "Hell no, lady. No way." Or, "There's not enough on the road to even bother about. The front's moved on east."

She was beginning to cry. Commencing, her grandmother would have said, commencing to cry. A characteristic archaic word that lent importance to the activity it modified and at the same time depersonalized it, like an affair of state. Troops commenced maneuvers, diplomats commenced discussions, and Louise commenced to cry. She could hear Grandma's quavery drawl.

She didn't want to go, that was it, because it wasn't a commencing at all, but an ending. Another leave-taking. Ciao, adios, sayonara, good-bye. The potential of this journey spent. Traveling, she left a trail behind her, pieces of herself, sectioned as though for a microscope, insubstantial, like holograms visible only from the proper perspective, each an infinitesimal diminution, leaving her ever slighter. If she turned back and retraced her steps she might reassemble like a deck of cards.

Someone was waiting for the phone, a teenager with a back-up battalion deployed throughout the convenience store. Louise blotted her face on her sleeve and looked him in the eye as she left the booth to him.

She turned around. Back in Park City the weather didn't seem so bad. It was hardly snowing. Perhaps it had only been an errant squall in the canyon. Maybe down on the flat she would have emerged into sunlight. Her faint heart reproached her.

No one was at the condominium. They'd said good-bye earlier when she loaded the Lincoln and left. It was an odd assortment of people Iris had assembled, none of them known to Louise. It had the makings of a farce or an episode of a sitcom, sharing space with strangers. They were out, at the movies or skiing, but she still had the key and let herself back in. She had the place to herself.

As the party's organizer Iris had determined the sleeping arrangements, assigned the beds, and had kept the master suite for herself. There was a tub in the adjoining bathroom, a swimming pool almost, sunken into the middle of the room. Louise ran it full and sank into water up to her chin. She felt like Goldilocks, an interloper, and imagined the clues to her presence she'd leave — a damp footprint on the mat, lingering humidity, a solitary hair. Later, when Iris returned, like the three bears she would exclaim, "Who's been cavorting in my tub?" It would be a disquieting mystery, never solved. They'd imagine a ghost or a former tenant who'd kept a key or they'd suspect each other like house party guests in an Agatha Christie novel. They wouldn't think of her. They'd seen her off, said good-bye.

Louise tried to calculate where she'd be now if she'd stayed on the road. Ogden, maybe, and beginning the climb toward the Idaho line. She was sorry she hadn't continued; there was nothing to return to in Park City. Her rout had been foolish. She was like a particle caught between two magnetic fields, or a satellite between gravitational forces. Los Angeles was exerting its pull, but the sortie down the canyon had disturbed her equipoise and over-balanced her in favor of home. She missed her boys, longed to recover herself in the routine of work and obligation. It was like waking from a dream. The weeks behind her seemed suddenly irresponsible, a dalliance, tainted by frivolity.

Louise stood up in the tub like a whale breaching.

thirteen

IN SALT LAKE the roads were bare and dry. If it had snowed at all it had been only a dusting.

At Twin Falls she wasn't tired yet, still alert at Boise. She drove on. In the middle of the night she headed up into the Blue Mountains outside of Baker and once again encountered snow. Motorists had holed up. There were no cars left on the road, only an occasional trailer truck and Louise.

The Lincoln's headlights, controlled by an electric eye, developed a mind of their own, automatically adjusting between high and low beam, blinking crazily at reflectors and warning signs as though sending coded messages, then failing to dim for taillights as Louise came up behind a truck until she was almost upon it.

She pulled out to pass and her lights clicked back onto high beam, flashing into the truck's side-view mirror as she drew parallel, and no way to express her chagrin. The truck accelerated and thundered alongside, throwing up a blinding curtain of snow. Louise hung onto the wheel and hurtled onward, tunneling into a wall of white, inching into the lead, like racing a locomotive. When she finally overtook the truck and pulled ahead, the driver turned on his own brights along with a spotlight mounted on the roof of the cab, like a gigantic Cyclops's eye, bathing the Lincoln in a wash of light. Louise imagined him drawing a bead on the back of her head with a rifle held in one hand.

The truck was right on her tail, gaining on her as the highway leveled. She could hear the rattle of its chains and the wail of the airhorn, a dragon in pursuit. She was already driving as fast as she dared, on the very edge of control, afraid to take her eyes off the road ahead even to check the mirrors.

Snow blew and eddied and the tires lost contact with the ice. She rounded a turn, her heart in her throat. She could imagine the car flipping, clearing the guard rail in a roll like a pole vaulter, spiraling like a football, snapping the tops of firs as it plunged into darkness.

She gave it more gas. The speedometer touched eighty. On the next curve she escaped the reach of the truck's lights and could see again. A blue sign flashed past, a viewpoint ahead. Behind her the spotlight went off. She was outrunning him.

Louise took the exit. She was going too fast, taking a chance, and the Lincoln spun twice around on the ramp as she braked, flattening her against the seat back, then came to a rocking halt. She hadn't hit anything. Out on the highway the trucked whipped past and Louise heard the blare of the horn doppler away into silence.

She was panting as though she'd outrun him on foot. A close call. She lit a cigarette and flipped on the dome light and searched the glove box for the manual in order to read about the headlights, but it wasn't there, just a map of west Texas and Mr. Swan's release.

It was three when she came down into Pendleton and it seemed too late by then to stop for a motel. The town was dark and muffled by snow, even the desk clerks would be sleeping. She didn't want to rouse someone and pay for a bed she'd only occupy for a few hours, and decided to travel on, but she headed west toward Portland instead of north in case weather might have closed the pass through the Cascades to Seattle. It was the long way home, but she'd have no more mountains to cross. Somewhere along the Columbia sleep overtook her and she pulled off the interstate onto a ranch road and collapsed sideways on the front seat under her coat. Snow accumulated on the windshield and she jolted awake in the faint first light inside a dim cocoon. Someone was tapping on the window.

She lurched upright behind the wheel. A face framed by cupped hands peered in at her through the glass, close enough to kiss, then withdrew. She was trying to remember, processing slowly. Her wits had exploded like pigeons off a roof, scattered, and now settled back, one by one. In a moment the adrenaline subsided, and the impulse to flee along with it. She recaptured her whereabouts. Her hand was on the key, but she only turned it part way and glided down the window.

The man tilted to look in at her again. "Everything okay?" he asked.

"I was tired," she said. "Asleep at the wheel. I just pulled off."

He shrugged and looked away into the distance. It was still snowing. "Yeah, well. Probably smart."

She smiled. "You startled me."

He smiled too. "Yeah, I saw that. But I thought, you know, some kind of trouble. You never know. Just checking, was all." His pickup was idling nearby, loaded with baled hay. On his way to feed cattle pastured somewhere beyond, she supposed. "Well," he said, "see you." He lifted his hand at her.

"Why do you say that?" she asked, suddenly peevish. "I'm going to drive off and you're *not* going to see me. I don't live here or anywhere near here." His face changed. He scratched the back of his head, tilting the visor of his cap lower over his eyes. Now he thought maybe she *was* some kind of trouble, drunk or deranged. She wondered why she'd said it. All the men, she supposed, vanished from her life. "Never mind," she said, and slid the window up between them.

By the time she reached The Dalles the snow had changed to rain and the Lincoln, its sides caked with dirty slush like a

127

lathered horse, the undercarriage burdened like a bomber's belly with a cargo of packed snow, was sluiced clean of evidence of the night's rigors.

At home nothing was familiar. Louise had no more sense of reunion with herself in the rooms of her house than she would have had upon returning to Moira's, say, or Mexico City, or to the hotel in Los Angeles, or to any other place once seen.

There was nowhere in the world, she thought, where she felt at home, no one place that rooted her, where she knew herself, though she remembered many houses and could draw mental floor plans, arrange the furniture, locate the windows and the views they gave onto. Sometimes she found herself doing it, going through some old house in her head, some-where she'd lived as a child or a wife, dollying like a camera down a narrow hall, mounting the stairs, panning rooms. But no matter how detailed and accurate the mental image, her recollections had proscenium limits like a stage or a picture cut off by the frame. Never enough. She wanted to go back, to knock on the door, explain herself, and accept an invitation to explore. But even then she'd find that too, inadequate. She longed to tumble back into the remembered time when the future was a blank potential, before it was written.

She tried to imagine her father prowling on some bedtime errand through the depths of his house in San Francisco, but she didn't know the house well enough, had never lived there, and couldn't follow him through the baffling warren of passages, stairs, and rooms. A wine cellar and a storage area they called the dungeon, full of old analytic couches and heir-loom rugs — treasures destined for her sister. The elevator, his office and the patients' waiting room, the heating plant, wher-ever *that* was. No doubt he could map the wiring and the pipes as well. He looked after his property carefully, thoroughly, ever responsible.

Her own house fell ever so gradually into a further state of disrepair. Dry rot weakened the stair treads on the porch, rain water spewed through split gutters and pooled along the foundation. She propped sash windows unevenly open with stacks of books. The floors were marred and the woodwork chipped down to old black varnish. The backyard fence sagged against the forsythia hedge. No Dutch girl she, with scrubbed stoop and pattens left at the door, everything scoured and tidy, with a convex mirror positioned to spy. No domesticated geraniums welcomed on her porch, but a tangle of clematis.

There were houses she'd seen, cat ladies' houses that children approached only on a dare or at Halloween, overgrown with brambles like Sleeping Beauty's bower. The shingles grew a thatch of moss where maple seedlings sprouted, and within the embrace of creepers the siding was spongy and porous. Perhaps one day hers would be such a house, and she its inhabitant, skittish and nocturnal object of pity and derision. Such a house would be, she thought, an external display of internal chaos and surrender. Perhaps then she'd feel at home.

She thought of her house as a single tiny bead strung on a remote line of northern latitude, a blip on a radar screen, a dot in a field of darkness. Years before she'd lived far out from a town in Wyoming off a county road that wound through folds of gently rising hills. At night, returning home, she could see the point of light that was her kitchen window like a low-hanging star for miles and miles as she approached, losing it sometimes, momentarily, behind the unseen shoulder of a hill. The light at once reassured and dismayed, evidence both of human habitation and of essential isolation.

It was like traveling as a child, lying in the coveted lower berth of a Pullman and staring out at the passage of a vast fabric of night pierced by an occasional remote and solitary light. Better to imagine those reaches uninhabited than to contemplate an existence of such estrangement. A welling up inside like an internal balloon inflating, a kind of reciprocal interior space, made it hard to catch her breath, like the beginning of a sob.

She imagined the life going on within the lit kitchen, a meal served, children bent over homework, dishes washed, as though outside the thin shell of the house there was not a wilderness of peril, as though the light itself conferred safety, like a ring of primitive fire holding tigers at bay. The bravado, though, of signaling your whereabouts, a sitting duck to marauders who might fix upon your star and approach in the dark undetected. Beside her in the berth her mother had slumbered, and beyond the curtain the porter padded the length of the car with a braced gait, but only window glass stood between Louise and the night.

But now the cat was pleased to see her, and Louise held it against her chest. The vibration of its purring was soothing, and when it sighed in contentment she felt a corresponding easing of strain. Years ago she'd been told that respirators were programmed to sigh, that even in a coma occasional suspiration was required.

The boys would come home from their father's house, and in time she'd reconstruct her routine of work and domestic chores. Louise imagined that from the street, behind a scrim of bare lilacs, lamps turned on against the rain-dark afternoon, her house gave the appearance of warmth and cheer, and maybe that was enough.

fourteen

THE LIGHT FROM the kitchen threw a little illumination down the basement stairs, elongated the shadows of the risers, failed to make the turn at the landing, but bounced some reflected light on down to the spot where Louise was sitting near the bottom of the steps. Her husband had used the basement as a woodworking shop, and fine red sawdust gave a nap to every surface, a slight blurring of edges like fur or fungus. His saws and planer were gone but the dust seemed self-perpetuating as though it filtered out of the rafters and hung in the air, a kind of ghostly insistence of his animus.

Louise had known the particular scream of each machine, the electric thrum of the motors that carried upstairs, the whir of blades; and each time she heard the shriek of metal biting into wood a charge stilled her heart until the cut was done as she waited for the human howl as a digit was severed, living out in imagination the scenario of emergency, blood-soaked rags and the finger packed in ice for the rush to the hospital.

Now the basement was vacant. The furnace spread its ducts overhead like an upended octopus or heavy-limbed tree. Shades were pulled over the half-windows to discourage prowlers in search of skis and bicycles or access to the house. Louise couldn't see them, but she knew that in the dark, in damp crevices or in the angles of joists, large brown spiders waited in attitudes of wary menace.

The basement was a sketchy archive of history, repository for tools and equipment — the beach umbrella, pipe wrench, lawn mower, Coleman stove, graduated sizes of skis and boots describing the advancing ages of the boys — articles whose occasional use conjured specific memories.

Louise sat on the step looking at two perfectly square smallish cardboard boxes which rested on a shelf between the studs of the basement wall. Like everything else, they were covered with a mantle of dust. She knew the contents, though one had never been opened, was still wrapped in the original plain paper.

There was a suspense about an unopened parcel, an added weight. When she was a girl feminine napkins still came wrapped in plain paper on the grocery shelves. She remembered demanding loudly and insistently to be told what was inside as she walked the aisles with her mother. Her mother tried to hush her with a kind of sad desperation, no match for Louise. Presents came in plain paper, gifts at birthdays and Christmas mailed by the generous absent grandmothers. Plain wrapping was a stratagem to divert interest which Louise had figured out.

In the car she was scolded. She had, her mother said, embarrassed her. It was something for women, grownups, nothing interesting and none of her business. Louise was steadfast and righteous. No explanation satisfied her. She was indignant that, having seen the parcel, she would not now be allowed to see its contents, a kind of protocol her mother had breached. Defeated, finally her mother relented. Louise opened the box as they drove. The layers of gauzy pads mocked her for her certainty. What're they *for*?

It was a complicated battle, she thought now, an assault mounted against her mother's wish to keep something to herself, and triumph left Louise with a disquieting intimation of her mother's pregnability.

She sighed. It was her mother in the box. A container of ash, all that was left. She could no longer really picture her mother. When she tried, someone else came to mind, someone she'd never known, her mother as a girl, Reeve Deason's girl, before she'd married, long before Louise, as she was in photographs, a lovely girl looking gravely into the camera and the future.

Louise didn't know what to do with the ashes. A genetic indecision, perhaps, for the other box contained her grandmother, her mother's mother, in a small brass urn. They hadn't liked each other, but there they were, inseparable in death, side by side on the basement shelf, carried through all the different moves, neither yet in a final resting place. She had thought of taking them to Edmonton — before they'd moved to Texas Louise's mother's side of the family was Canadian — where her grandfather was buried, or his ashes interred, she didn't know which. But looking at a map she'd been daunted. A trip to Edmonton wouldn't be just a little jaunt east on 90, it was a long way north as well. If she'd been thinking she might have taken them to Texas, pulled off the road somewhere and let them go on the wind. But a solemnity would have been wanting. She might have felt furtive, as though illegally dumping refuse.

M.'s mother was still alive. Twice a year he went to visit her, or more perhaps, some years, if his schedule allowed. He showed Louise a photograph once, an old black-and-white snapshot he carried in his wallet of him and his mother. It was faded and indistinct and Louise couldn't make out the child he had been, or see the mother's face. She wondered why he carried it, what it was about that particular hazy image he treasured. It was taken indoors and from his size it would have been toward the end of the war. A seated woman in a long dark dress, and a boy standing near her in a room that might have been a kitchen. Illumination from a window divided the photograph diagonally into halves of light and shadow. Louise wished she'd asked what the occasion was that had led to the photograph being taken and preserved. The figures appeared solemn, neither festive nor formal, watchful, as though listening to a bombardment or a broadcast. Normandy perhaps, the tremors or the announcement of the invasion, aircraft lumbering overhead, the concussion of ordnance, or Churchill's ponderous voice.

Louise envied M.'s mother who had, by her presence alone, not through any entreaty, the power to summon him. When he spoke of visiting her it sounded as though obligation moved him, that he went to fulfill a responsibility, but that degree of fealty to duty wasn't in his nature. The submission to responsibility was itself an expression of the singular place his mother had in his heart. There was a poignancy in the idea of him so governed, like the nape of the neck or the inside of the wrist, an unconscious vulnerability.

Louise tried to imagine his arrival and their greeting. The mother waiting, listening for his taxi, an engine idling in the street while he paid, then his key in the lock. The twin horns of delight his visits would spike into her mental calendar.

Louise had seen photographs of his daughters, too. School pictures, head shots in color. Pretty girls, teenagers, barely older than her own sons, moving away, creating their own lives. Louise thought he let them go with relief, yielding to boyfriends eager to supplant him, as though as the girls became more complex his love subsided.

In her imagination Louise was able to place herself on either side of him, to conjure up the feelings of a mother or a daughter, to lay claim to all varieties of love. She yearned for a position for herself like theirs that would ensure his affection, the bliss of unearned love.

She saw him, as though she'd lived it, at a beach, sitting in the dunes with a child in his lap, hero and protector, the girl's bare legs and sandaled feet straddling him, lying back inside his loose embrace while his attention focused elsewhere, laughing with other adults while the child leveled her complacent gaze on the world from her position of security and favor.

At home, going about real life, Louise was a stranger, a visitor from another planet, or like Venus, emerging fully-formed on a foreign shore where she didn't speak the language or know the customs, proceeding in perpetual bewilderment. Or Rip Van Winkle, awakening from her marriage like a long coma to an altered world, unprepared for changes that had occurred in her absence. She didn't belong. It was like being sick as a child and missing something in school, the nines table, say, and ever after feeling slightly out of step as though she'd come in late on life.

She greeted each day startled as she woke anew to this dislocation. Divorce had divested her of identity. She was lost without the fixed reference of marriage like a pole star to locate her in the galaxy. She was unable to recall degrees of intimacy and their attendant rituals of behavior. She might seem strangely cool or inappropriately familiar. Nixon, she'd heard, betrayed guilt or madness by swinging his arms out of rhythm as he walked, having to concentrate on a function that should be native. Her own smile felt stiff on her face and her sentences rang false as though they were nonsense, gibberish. She thought people looked at her with pity or suspicion and might talk about her in her absence. She bought Raybans with black lenses to conceal a gaze that might be shifty or fixed. Normal as she might appear exchanging pleasantries with a neighbor or with the checker at the grocery store, she was observing rote conventions, like a pod person, a clever decoy.

There was no sense of malice from the world at large, just an inability to penetrate it. It made her feel furtive, wary of scrutiny as though she were incognito. She longed for night, for the cover of darkness when her deviance was less discernible, when the children were home from school, the neighborhood filled again, and her presence had an equal

135

legitimacy. During the days she felt truant and guilty and refrained from the pleasures she might have enjoyed, daytime baths or naps, and imprisoned herself at her desk.

Sometimes she found herself totally vacant as if she had departed momentarily in a seizure or a fit, like a red-haired girl she'd gone to grade school with who emerged from epileptic spasms to find all eyes upon her in a kind of polite suspension. Louise thought people looked at her oddly in the grocery store or the post office and she wondered if she'd spoken aloud, and tried to remember her last thought to determine what she might have said.

She knew she was inflating one aspect of her life out of all proportion until the disparity between the actuality of M. and his importance to her was lunatic. She wondered if she was losing her mind. Her life was built up on a pediment of fiction. He had the same function and no more substance than a child's imaginary playmate, an invisible presence she fabricated as armor against the world.

This impairment was capricious and sometimes vanished, or lay dormant, like a toggle turned off, allowing her to feel herself again and at home in the world, and then she wondered if it might be some hormonal imbalance, an infusion like a virus. She tried to fix a pattern to it like you might if plagued by headache, to determine what keyed its onset: chocolate or brie or Southern Comfort in her coffee.

The children, Louise believed, didn't notice. She was a fixture to them, reliably present, and their predictable appearances after school and at supper, their requests for her attention and interest, anchored the afternoons and brought her thudding back from the ozone.

Sometimes — rarely, but sometimes — when the sense of unreality became intolerable, Louise called M. At the other end of the line his assistant's cheerful recognition of her voice rendered the call mundane and deflated its magnified importance. It suddenly seemed simple and ordinary to telephone him, and the relationship telescoped back to normal proportions. Beforehand she had imagined a blank pause when she said her name, a rebuff to an unwelcome caller. Some psycho on the line dogging an idol.

But their conversations were brief and censored by the presence of his assistant, reduced to commonplaces. Afterwards Louise mentally replayed each sentence, trying to find a message of affection or promise.

Occasionally M. telephone her from his empty house on a weekend afternoon when his family was out or late at night from a hotel somewhere when he was traveling or on location.

She'd read an account of ordinary women — secretaries, nurses, retail clerks — who came home from their day jobs to roommates or boyfriends or to empty apartments, and later, after supper and dishes and walking the dog, they talked sex for hire on a nine hundred line. Louise imagined a tired woman in her bathrobe in an upstairs bedroom where an ironing board was perpetually set up in the corner. She did her nails perhaps, sitting cross-legged on the bed, or rolled her hair, or stood at the ironing board with the phone cradled in her shoulder, pressing a dress for tomorrow's work while she murmured salacious scenarios into her caller's ear and mimed the fast shallow breathing of arousal. Louise tried to imagine the fantasies she called upon, and the words she used, the descriptions of tumescence, slippery orifices and penetration, postures of submission and dominance. The image appealed to Louise. She liked the discrepancy of engagement, the caller panting toward his climax while the woman maneuvered the iron around collar and cuffs. It didn't seem as though it would be difficult. The phone would release you from your inhibitions and you could turn over a rock in your mind to expose hidden carnal worms.

But when M. called from bed in a distant hotel with his penis in his hand Louise came up to it like a horse to a wall and balked, tongue-tied and bashful.

"What are you wearing?" he wanted to know. "Where's your hand? What are you thinking?"

"I can't do this," she said.

"Yes, you can. Don't you masturbate?"

"Sometimes I do."

"So, what do you do? What do you think about?"

"I don't know," she said.

"Tell me." It was like falling backwards and believing he'd catch her. She didn't think she could do it. "Do you think of a woman, or being watched, tied up, two at once? Tell me your fantasy."

"Just imagine," she said, "what I'd do if I were there."

"What?" he persisted.

"You know."

"Say it."

"No." He waited. "I can curl my tongue," she said finally, and laughed, an absurd non sequitur popping into mind, some sort of innate diversionary tactic. "Roll it up like a cigar. It's genetics, like Mendel's peas."

He laughed. "And?"

"And nothing."

"Do what with it?"

There was a silence. What did it matter? She closed her eyes. "I sit on you," she whispered. "I lower myself down onto you. You slide up inside me. I'm wet and tight and we watch it go in. I won't let you move. Only me, just a little bit so the head of your cock rubs where I like it where it's soft and slick like a bruise in a peach. I make you stay still and look in my eyes. Or you can watch my hand. I slide a finger in up alongside your penis and stroke it and you like the way that feels

138

and I bring it out wet and play with myself. Faster and faster. You're watching. I rise up and you slide out of me all wet and thick until just the tip is still inside then I sink down and you're hard and big and it feels like you go all the way up to my throat and we roll over so you're on top and I hold your balls while you come."

M.'s wordless cry of climax rocketed her instantly to where he was. A long bravura wail that might as easily signal anguish, like the baritone's bellow at the close of a Mahler song. Afterwards, for a moment, with his breath in her ear, Louise could almost imagine he was beside her.

Later she heard trains. Always at night she wakened to the rumble of a southbound freight on the Burlington Northern tracks down along the waterfront, the squeal of shunted cars and the concussion of coupling, sound waves rolling uphill from the switching yard like billows of smoke. Neighbors complained and citizens' committees formed to fight the noise, fearing reduced property values, but Louise liked the nocturnal disturbances, atavistic as a wolf's howl. She thought of trains across Texas, across the continent, the conduits of connection her family once traveled, every summons — sickness, death, celebration — all answered by rail, all conventions observed.

Net hung from her grandmother's hat as she embarked on journeys and foxes chased each other around her shoulders in perpetual pursuit and capture, jaws clamped onto paws, tails dangling. Underneath her wool crepe suit boned undergarments and elastic hose encased her in a fortress of probity. A lace jabot contained her wattles and gloves stilled her palsied hands. Like a Crusader armored for battle with no inch of bare skin exposed. Without the external fortifications she'd melt like candle wax. Behind the curtain in the berth at night she took it all off and put it back on again in the morning underneath the tent of her nightdress.

In the dining car of the City of San Francisco when she was sixteen, Louise ordered tea and clamped the lemon wedge between her fingers for eleven hundred miles, thinking she'd bleach the nicotine stain, afraid to face her father. On the return she necked all night with a soldier in the observation car. He put his tongue in her mouth and in her ear and unbuttoned her blouse and pinched her nipples. At dawn his hand was up under her skirt and Louise watched the shadows of their heads race across the prairie, rippling into a tangle of antelope legs as a band of pronghorns ran beside the train, while he brought her off, astonishing them both.

Turning alone in bed Louise was heavy, ponderous, as though with a slowed pulse like a bear in winter. In the shower she felt her body, so alive under M.'s hands, dead beneath her own. Like soaping a corpse, she thought, as she sponged her thighs. From habit she continued rituals of optimism — at night stroked cream into her face to slow the lines, ran three miles on alternate days, and gave up smoking.

At her desk work progressed slowly. She stared dreamily out the window for long stretches. Each afternoon at twilight a tattered streamer of crows crossed the sky like noisy scraps of torn felt or blown leaves, hundreds upon hundreds of them along a flyway to the southwest. Louise thought they must be flying to roost, but she wondered where they came from, where they spent their days, what fallow inland fields. Unlike commuters, which they otherwise resembled, they didn't reverse the performance in the mornings. Perhaps it was a miracle, an origination — leaves torn loose and animated by the afternoon zephyr into crows.

fifteen

MARION'S WILL WAS probated. The Lincoln was Louise's. Along with the title, her father sent a note reminding her that the car was his gift, not Marion's bequest. Some careless remark of hers prompting the admonition.

She had supposed that if it became officially hers she'd trade for something else, for a second-hand Volvo station wagon, safe and practical, but she discovered that she'd attached herself to the Lincoln, fallen for it like a woman for an illicitly adopted child, the bond emphatically and prematurely cemented by the possibility of having to give it back. Now she decided she would keep it. But in the security of possession she looked at it with altered eyes, saw its ungainly length and boxy lines and was mildly embarrassed to be identified with it. At the same time, once it was hers it became commonplace, ordinary, simply her car, her transportation, the way she got around, and she thought less and less about it. She wondered if M.'s allure was like the Towncar's, predicated on the tenuousness of connection, not on anything inherent in him. If he weren't married, if she might win him, perhaps she wouldn't care. She might find the affair burdensome, tedious, desire diminished by legitimacy.

Louise flew once again to Midland, a last journey to Texas to help pack and disperse the household belongings which Marion had left to her father. A second reunion with her family. They met her at the airport, her father and Julia and her brother. Anne couldn't get away, a doctor, with larger claims against her time.

Louise folded herself into the back seat of the rented car beside Leland, territory once divided by an imagined meridian and jealously guarded against a sibling's encroachment, even so much as a finger over the line was an affair of state, required parental intervention — "He's over on *my* side." The squabbles of childhood. Now she had nothing but fondness for him.

The sun fell across the pale prairie with a pulsing glare like the onset of a migraine. Louise was cold and her tongue tasted metallic, like Sensen. What was that, she wondered, anise seed or something similar that her boyfriend had carried years ago instead of cigarettes? It was like returning to the scene of a crime. Her memory of being there previously was more powerful than the present moment.

They passed through the gate of the nursing home where Grandma had died and Faye still lived, if you could call it that, but turned away into an adjoining retirement complex and wound along a curving street, designed, Louise supposed, in defiance of the logic of a grid on the plane of prairie, contours intended to suggest non-existent topography.

Marion's was a low brick house with overhanging eaves and a wide front door approached by a ramp. Preparedness for infirmity. Here you could get around with a cane or a walker, or in a wheelchair, and finally on a gurney. No stairs for the aged to assault like climbers on Everest — step, breathe, step again.

Inside, the rooms looked ransacked. Large pieces of furniture were set at peculiar angles, tables and chairs buried under papers and articles of clothing. It seemed impossible that Marion, an orderly man, had lived in this disarray. You could chart his habits like following animal signs in the woods, bent twigs and a hair caught in the bark of a tree clues to trails and habitats. A computer was set up on a door on legs like a student's desk beneath a bank of sagging board-and-bracket shelves, everything within arm's reach so you wouldn't have to move. On the couch an open spot surrounded by cushions and printouts and periodicals, and everywhere telephones, ashtrays, empty glasses, and remote controls for the television sets. Chairs were strategically placed along the pathways between door jams, their backs like notches on a climbing wall positioned to aid hand-over-hand progress through the rooms on the way to the bathroom or the kitchen.

Standing still in the chill chaos of Marion's living room in a moment that might have acknowledged his departure and their trespass, it didn't appear that they would discover a single article of value or interest.

When her mother died Louise sold the entire contents of the house unsorted to a secondhand dealer who walked through and gave her a bid chiseled to nothing by the prospect of dump fees and haulage. Trash, he said, she should pay *him*. She kept the butterfly collection and the bone china that had come down from the English forebears, and nothing else.

One kitchen drawer was an archive of preserved tinfoil, saved and re-used, washed and smoothed out again until worn into irregular shapes pleated and pliable as Fortuny silk, and still used again to wrap a tiny scrap of something or to fold over an open tin can, until it was finally layered onto a wad of foil that grew gradually from a pea size to a golf ball, then into a basketball, a giant watermelon of compressed tinfoil. What did you do with that? Louise's mother saved cottage cheese containers and yogurt cups, jars, rubber bands, and the foil trays from a diet of frozen pot pies. The linen closet was filled with grayed and tattered towels, scraps of towels, yellowed sheets, diapers even, relics from infancy, enough rags to bandage an army. Louise's mother bought the bottom of the line, shopped from Sears by catalogue, treated herself to nothing, measured character by adversity, worth by deprivation. Whatever aesthetic she possessed was vanquished before her rampaging thrift. Upon her death the second-hand dealer swept away an entire household that bore witness to the perversion of a virtue into pathology. Marion's house brought her mother's flooding back.

The enormity of the task before them and their shared distaste for it united them. They exchanged glances and made small inarticulate noises of dismay. Louise felt again the cheering cohesion she'd experienced in San Antonio — in hostile territory the tribe embraced even its least member.

Julia turned up the thermostat. Louise looked in the refrigerator: a bottle of Galliano and a jar of olives. Leland strapped a box into shape from the scored cardboard the moving company had provided. Like a lizard warming in the sun, a locomotive building steam, they bestirred themselves.

In theory it had seemed simple enough. Sort things into two piles, box the breakables and the moving company would do the rest, ship east and west, to Boston and Sacramento, to Anne and Leland. Louise, having the Lincoln, so much more valuable than a bureau or a television or the ball-and-talon-footed table, was not expected to want anything else and was thus relieved of avarice. She was only there to assist.

Julia had to act as Anne's agent, consulting with her long distance, describing, measuring, guessing weight and value. The moving company charged a flat rate for the first one thousand pounds, but after that there was an additional per-hundred-pound charge. It was doubtful that much of what Anne thought she wanted was worth the cost of shipping. Sight unseen, based on Julia's telephoned descriptions, Anne wanted many heavy things — a dark oak library table with pineapple legs, the matching chair, a sideboard, the computer, chests of drawers, and, incomprehensibly, the refrigerator. For the basement, she said, to store film and beer. Leland tipped it forward against his shoulder. Two hundred pounds, he said. One big man. More, Louise thought; twice that.

Louise sipped Galliano from an eyecup while she scoured the inside of the refrigerator. Julia's idea, cleaning it before shipping it, ever alert to Anne's interests.

On the shelves above the computer, Leland's discovery, a book of beautifully reproduced Japanese erotic paintings. They took turns paging through the plates. No way of knowing what went through anyone else's mind looking at the astonishing anatomy, the contortions, and the impassive faces of the depicted lovers. If you wanted, Louise thought, it would function as a kind of Rorschach. You'd reveal yourself by your description of what was going on — not physically, for that was clear — but the circumstances of the encounters, the relationships between the participants, and the roles of furtive attendant figures. Louise searched for it later, thinking she'd take it with her and show it sometime to M., but it was gone. She wondered which one of her family had made off with it.

In the afternoon Louise walked into the wind along the curving street to the nursing home while the others drove. As well as dismantling Marion's house they had to empty Grandma's room and a storage locker across town.

In every respect, except that the bed was stripped, the room looked the same as when Louise had last seen it, but it was occupied now by a vacancy like silence, an absence of anything kinetic, as though habitation set off invisible tremors. Like violin wood, its cellular structure altered by play, the room unused, was flat, without volume or resonance.

Julia went through Grandma's dresser drawers. Fossilized cake carried back to the room from some long-ago meal as a treat for the Little Boy, Hattie's imaginary child, and hidden in the lingerie among yellowed nylon gowns and shapeless tap pants. But Julia remembered pearls, an amethyst ring, Grandma's wedding band, stickpins and lavalieres, all missing, lost, misplaced, given away, or, as Julia thought, stolen by nurses or aides. People who employed servants, Louise thought, prized honesty in proportion to their dependence on it. A maid's principles, or her caution, protected Julia, and she revealed her vulnerability in her quick suspicion. Here querulous old women lost credibility and you could throw caution to the wind, leaving only principles hanging on an aide like raiments, decking her out like ermine and silk so she looked you square in the eye, as good as anyone. Grandma might have given the amethyst away, lost the wedding band down a drain, the pearls could have been vacuumed up from under the dresser, rattling up the hose in a cocoon of slut's wool. Or, to be sure, everything might repose now in a leatherette box on someone else's bureau, dusted with spilled talc in a room that smelled of Evening in Paris, jewels worn out to church or for a night at the Glo Room, but never worn to work. Louise didn't want to know.

Julia took the photograph of Louise's father down from the wall for Anne, but they left Faye hanging there. In the photograph her lip curved a little off center in an effort to cover her teeth so that she looked like she was supressing a smile.

They looked in on the real Faye as they left, but she was sleeping, curled on her side facing away from the door, and they went away without waking her. Leaving the likeness behind seemed both a symbol and an omen and Louise suddenly wanted to go back, retrieve it, trick herself and any watching spirits into believing in good intentions, believing that she'd be back, that Faye was in good hands, as cherished as her photograph.

146

Julia reconnoitered the corridors like a platoon leader each time before stepping out, afraid of encountering the nurse, Ella, who was God-only-knew-what to Marion, though if she was everything Louise's family presumed her to be she'd fared badly in the will. He'd left her a refrigerator, not the good one now destined for Anne, but an old one out in the garage, rounded like a fender, and a leaf blower, enigmatic in the tree-less reaches of west Texas. Marion died at home. Ella had found him. A dark night that would have been, after a blazing late summer for them both. Julia wanted to avoid Ella's grief and ire.

The storage locker was on the other side of town, south of the tracks. The squalor zone, a friend called the fringe where settlement blended into pasture, where people kept horses, burned their trash in oil drums, and parked fleets of cars in the front yards. It was nearly dusk when they got there. A low U, like a barracks, built around a dusty parade ground where trucks could maneuver. Like breaking into a pharaoh's tomb, wresting off the hasp with a crow bar, prying open the door, but inside there was only more old furniture and stacked card-board cartons covered with a layer of silt. "Keepsakes," Grandma had written, but nothing in the contents retained any meaning for anyone else.

The wind was cold. Julia stayed in the car. Louise watched the sky darken and close down overhead, sucked in tight by all the stashed memories.

Afterwards, they crawled through the cafeteria line at Luby's, an establishment made famous by random violence in another Texas town, and Louise thought about Filene and a pickup crashing through plate glass and the rat-a-tat-tat of gunfire, food and corpses.

In the morning the movers came for Anne's shipment. Two Hispanic men, wary and deferential, who took pains as though they'd been briefed, cautioned by their boss to beware the grandee. The refrigerator went last. The family watched the truck lumber away, a heavy load. Anne would pay for her treasures.

Julia turned to Louise's father. "I wonder —-you don't suppose it went with the house, do you?" Louise knew instantly what she meant. The thought didn't seem to originate with Julia, but in Louise's own mind, as though they'd thought it at the same moment, shared it telepathically, or she'd known it all along. The almond-colored refrigerator, fitted neatly into a niche in the matching almond cabinets, was as patently a part of the house as the kitchen sink, property of the retirement community. In all the discussion of the refrigerator — color, dimensions, age, condition — it had never occurred to them to wonder if it was theirs to take. They filed into the kitchen and looked at the space where the refrigerator had been. Like a wound, a hole left by a molar. "Well," Louise's father murmured.

Louise laughed. The unlikeliness of it, the unwieldiness of the plunder, the contradiction of a hot refrigerator, like elements in a farce, genteel slapstick like *The Lady Killers,* her family cast as improbable crooks.

Mr. Swan was coming, needing something signed. He'd notice, Julia worried. "Maybe we should put boxes there, make it less noticeable." A packing barrel to fill the hole, crumpled paper to distract the eye, compounding the crime with the cover-up. Louise thought they should call the moving company, intercept the truck, get it to turn around, but her father seemed unconcerned. Louise was learning another side of him.

148

Mr. Swan was like a toy man, Tin Tin or the groom off a wedding cake, miniature and precise, craning his neck to look up at Louise's father, his head tipped back so far Louise worried that the toupee would drop off. When he turned to her he inquired how the trip to San Francisco in the Lincoln had gone, irony in his eyes. "Fine," she said, "Uneventful." But she blushed. There'd been a parking ticket in Los Angeles, neglected too long and forwarded to the bank, then on to her father. By the time it reached her she'd paid the fine, but the paper trail betrayed her. Mr. Swan knew she'd been traveling other roads, but he smiled anyway, old friends.

They sat in the living room on what was left of the furniture. Louise's father signed the documents, then there was silence, the practiced silence of psychiatrists, a vessel waiting to be filled. Mr. Swan was tempted but cautious, a coyote circling a trap. Louise saluted him. He wanted to linger, she could see that. He had nothing to go home to and their tall family closed over him like a canopy. But he was wounded and afraid they'd scent his blood and turn on him. He shook hands all around and took his leave.

Louise walked him out. A Russian thistle tumbled in the street like a movie prop, cinematic shorthand for desolation. She stood on the curb looking up at the sky while he went around the car and opened his door. "Well," he said, and then reached suddenly across the roof. Normally Louise shook hands firmly, gripping like a man, but this time she gave him her hand softly like a little animal to hold for a moment before he got quickly into the car.

She watched as he pulled away. He'd said nothing of the purloined refrigerator.

One summer, visiting Midland as a child, Louise had two cousins who hadn't been there before — wiry tough boys older than she was who impressed her with an air of vice and disdain. They knew stickball and kick-the-can, exotic urban games. Their knuckles were swollen and etched with dirt. They led her through alleys and empty lots, loping along like dogs on patrol, chigger-bitten ankles and foxtails stuck in their socks. Kenny had a bruised handsome face like Audie Murphy's that captured Louise's sympathy, and Ray's was sharp as a rodent's.

They dropped away as they had come, into some void of pique and misfortune, unmourned except perhaps by Faye. Kenny had eventually resurfaced, a career navy man in marine refrigeration stationed in San Diego, and he'd come to Marion's funeral, Louise's father reported, was cordial and showed pictures of his wife and daughters. But he was aggrieved again when the will was read. He got only the silverware and whatever else was left in the house when they were through. Worse, Louise thought, to inherit their leavings than nothing at all, like a picked-over fire sale. No wonder he was mad. And they were leaving a mess. She wanted to straighten up, arrange the remaining furniture into a semblance of a home, tidy drawers, erase the evidence of pillage, save his feelings. She lived, she thought, inside two skins, always climbing into someone else's shoes.

With Anne's truckload underway, their father and Julia left Louise and her brother to finish up. When it was done Leland dropped Louise at the airport while he returned the rental car. She waited at the curb with her bag at her feet and Marion's shotguns under her arm.

She'd found the guns in the closet by the front door, back in the corner behind the leaf blower and a nylon windbreaker on a wire hanger, propped in the corner, not in their cases. Nothing colder than gun barrels, yet almost alive. As soon as she touched them Louise wanted them.

"Oh, no," Julia wailed when she saw them, turning away, shielding her eyes as though even looking was perilous. But Louise's father was interested. He lifted one, held it in front of him on flat palms as though inspecting fabric, weighed it, turned it in his long white physician's hands. His impulse, Louise was sure, inhibited by Julia, was to raise it to his shoulder. You never lost the feel for a gun, were born with it, perhaps.

"Can I have them?" Louise asked, avid, quickly, before Leland could speak. "For the boys," she added, endowing the request with a masculine sanction. She wasn't sure why she wanted the guns so badly. She might never shoot them herself, but she wanted the weight, the precision and workmanship, wanted them intrinsically, for what they were.

"Sure," her father said.

"I don't like them having guns," Julia objected. Her fear was primitive, uninformed, not so much that a gun might be turned against her, but more general, as though guns were capable of independent malice.

At the airport, waiting, Louise felt drawn up and separate, as though she wore her skeleton on the outside like an insect. Carrying the guns, she turned heads. People stared. In Texas, she thought, she was always looking like something she was not. Now she looked like a sportswoman back from dove hunting down on the Brazos, someone you might think you recognized from the society page, a tycoon's wife or senator's daughter.

There was difficulty checking the guns and a delay while Louise negotiated, then a last-minute flurry, running for the gate with only moments to spare. The guard let Leland through security with a thirty-inch fish poacher that hadn't fit into any of the boxes, but confiscated a garden trowel he had tucked into his back pocket. They laughed as they sprinted for the plane, unlikely terrorists, thinking of salmon and dill.

There was a softened regard in the way people looked at them that acknowledged their resemblance to each other — clearly brother and sister, not husband and wife — and approved, an affection free of the tincture of sex. They sat in seats facing each other behind the bulkhead of the small plane and watched Midland fall away.

Louise didn't think her brother would choose her for a friend, or that they'd have known each other in another life, but born to each other as they were, they were cemented. Between siblings the bond, if there was one, was as mysterious as any other, just some shared chemistry, molecules in synchrony. Louise would have said it was memory, a shared past, except that her brother remembered nothing. She had tried leading him back, Gretel on the trail of bread crumbs, prompting him with details, but something had shut him off from the past they shared as though a door had dropped or she'd dreamed herself a brother. He was a geneticist with amnesia. He spent his life on family ties, but couldn't remember his own.

They had a drink between Midland and El Paso, and another between El Paso and Phoenix, where Leland had to change for Sacramento. He kissed her good-bye, bent awkwardly in the aisle, the fish poacher under his arm, and called her Lou like he used to do when they were children.

sixteen

A MORNING SOMETIMES, something in the air — if something happened, a catastrophe, an earthquake or a fire, or if you met the man you later married, you'd say it was a premonition, that you'd felt it coming, had known on waking.

The air was still, heavy, already warm and promising heat, air with presence and density, like scent or fluid, an element at body temperature. It was like waking in the tropics, somewhere foreign. Like waking from a magical slumber, too, sleep without memory in which you might have been transported. No idea upon waking of what lay out the window, beyond the door, or in which direction you'd find the bathroom, who you were, even — sleep that deep. Like Dorothy in Oz, your wits suspended.

Louise cast back. To reassure herself of sanity she wanted to remember without visual clues. It was coming back.

To get to Midland you had to dog-leg somewhere. Louise had arranged her flights to Texas and back to connect through Los Angeles with a few days' layover on the return. When Leland left her in Phoenix she had continued on.

But it was a jinxed sojourn, she feared, the stars out of alignment, Mercury in retrograde. Los Angeles was a teeming city, full of millions and millions of anonymous souls, where you might search forever and never encounter a friend. But her first night in town, parking her rented Taurus, a generic car, invisible, she would have thought, at a meter in front of M.'s office building, Louise had heard her name called. Across the street in the opposite lane, blocking traffic until the light changed, was Iris, waving and calling out. It seemed impossible that she should have seen Louise, or having seen her, registered her as anything more than a profile glimpsed in the dusk that looked familiar but couldn't be placed and that might nag like a bar of music playing in your head until you could put the words to it. Louise felt exposed, too far from cover, Bambi's mother out in the meadow.

Iris had turned sideways and rested her arms along her car window like a backyard gossip and called above the noise of traffic, "Louise!" drawn out in her leisurely Tennessee drawl, conversationally. "What are you doing here?" Her voice carried without stridency and she was unflustered by honking behind her. "Why didn't you call me? I didn't know you were in town. Where are you going?" Dropping her final G's. Louise had heard the warmth in her voice, and the invitation. Iris wanted to park and join up. Louise had felt a sweat breaking.

"I *will* call you," she had shouted. "I'll call you tomorrow." She sounded evasive, she knew, a bad actress telegraphing. She could hear it herself. Iris had shrugged and waved, but pulled a knowing face as she shifted gears and moved on.

Louise had sat still for a moment, shaken, her hand to her mouth. She wondered if she'd blown her cover, if Iris would put things together, read the signs backwards, remember hints or evasions, disappearances. If she thought about it she'd remember where M.'s office was. She might have met him here herself. What now? Louise wished she'd dodged out into the street, kissed her. "What fun to see you. How extraordinary, don't you think?" Tapped her watch. "I'm rushing, I've got something now, but I'll call you tomorrow. We'll have lunch." Waving, smiling, hurrying off in the wrong direction, puffing up a smoke screen. Or the truth, even, probably the best tactic. "Guess who I'm meeting — M., you remember him, you introduced us, remember? We're having a drink. Come! Come with me. It'll be fun." Brash and confident, nothing to hide.

Shit, she thought, she should have done *something* differently.

Later Louise had wondered if Iris had parked after all, followed her up the street to the Mirabelle and seen M. waiting, seen them greet and kiss. Because when Louise had telephoned the next day she'd never asked anything more about the encounter, it wasn't mentioned, dropped as though forgotten.

Now, waking, Louise remembered that she was in Los Angeles in a strange hotel where she'd never been before. The usual hotel was booked, she couldn't get in, a convention of distributors in town. The Château, a Hollywood favorite, had had one small room left, high up in the angle of an ell, and Louise took it. There weren't any suites. She didn't care but she felt compromised and apologetic telephoning to tell M.

But once there, in the room, Louise's spirits had grown wings. She hadn't known, had never realized, how oppressed she'd felt before in their usual hotel where the rooms were spacious horizontally, huge beds with acres to roam, but no headroom, as though a gigantic weight bore down from above compressing space and air, flattening you into a squat shape like a fun-house mirror, or bending you double, Atlas with the world on your back. Here her spirits soared. Room to stand en pointe and reach your arms above your head, leap if you wished, and still not touch the ceiling.

A French door opened onto a stone balcony and the close black arms of a Monterey cypress, so near there were needles underfoot, and below lay Sunset Boulevard with its parade of billboards like giant playing cars set on edge marching toward the sea, and the strut and rumpus of traffic snaking between Hollywood and Beverly Hills.

M. hadn't liked the room. Louise was disappointed. She'd thought that like her he'd feel more at home. There was, she realized, so much she'd never know and could only guess. Attitudes and preferences. She could only partially surmise him from clues and inferences. Her relationship with him was circumscribed in a way that was instructive, like a microcosm of a larger truth. No one could ever have free range in another's heart and mind, yet the conventions of intimacy suggested that possibility. M. insisted upon separateness. He wouldn't accept her, so she could not bestow herself. There was a liberation, like weightlessness, in embracing desire without conditions. Expectations, the ideas of possession or power, floated off like detritus from a spaceship. Leaving him free, she was free herself.

M. was tired. He'd been sick and his face was drawn and pale. Louise thought that already she could see him age. In only the time she'd known him his face was thinner. She held his head when he kissed her, felt the rock of his skull between her hands, the smallness, really, of his head, not like any head she'd held before, and thought that there between her palms she held a universe of imagination, and all he'd lived and dreamed. Whales, she'd heard, each individual whale, knew the entire species' lore — currents, feeding grounds, songs, history if they had one — this phenomenon demonstrating, she was told, the infinite intelligence of whales, a capacity for data so much greater than our own. But did they dream, Louise wondered, as her M. did?

They lay on the bed with the light on, kissing with their eyes open, taking their time. Louise didn't think his eyes could lie, only that she misread what she saw there. She didn't suppose it was love, but didn't know another word for it. With him she felt grown, an adult. Life was a long act of separation, a cleavage, the gulf widening. They were, she thought, like channel swimmers, assaulting different shores, a surprise meeting in lonely waters, clinging together for a moment.

Later, Louise had watched M. through the open bathroom door. He was naked, his skin sallow against the salmon tiles, his penis sweetly hanging against his leg. He braced his arms against the sink and bowed his head as though in pain or indecision. Louise suddenly feared for his heart. He looked at her and she thought he wanted to say something. She looked away, afraid to hold his eye. Whatever he'd say could as easily be a declaration of love or a farewell. She didn't want to hear it.

Later M. sat beside her on the bed. He smiled, but was silent, and Louise thought of all the things she'd like to hear him say, all the lies another man would tell. She was beautiful, he loved her, he'd leave his wife, everything would be all right. But he wouldn't tell the truth, either. That it had been nice, despite the room, that he'd think of her, he'd call, she'd see him again.

"So?" he said, and smiled.

"So."

A long look, and a kiss at the door.

When he left Louise walked out onto the balcony and from six stories above waited for him to drive away. There was a long lag — the elevator, she supposed, and then the parking valet locating his car — before she saw him pull out of the garage directly below, slip down the steep drive, then hairpin onto Sunset. He would never think to look up. She'd be gone already from his mind, his thoughts onto something else. She imagined his drive home and could picture every turn until she lost him somewhere near the top of Beverly Glen.

Now, in the morning, his smell was still beside her in the bed. Her sense of place regained, the geography of the room recalled, Louise ordered coffee, and when it came carried it out onto the balcony. A haze over the city whitened the sky, dimmed the sun in an eerie semblance of an eclipse, like a portent, stilling birdsong. From where she sat Louise could see billboard painters down below hanging in buckets above Sunset, like a high wire act or performance art staged for her benefit, tiny human figures dangling before an enormous painted sky. So L.A. The aniline blue made a more convincing firmament than the actual sky which framed it like a gauzy proscenium.

Louise had thought that billboard signs were giant collages, sections of a photograph hung like wallpaper. She hadn't realized, or hadn't thought about it enough to realize, that the advertisements along Sunset were actually gigantic painted canvases, remnants of a vanishing art. She wondered how the painters kept perspective. Perhaps it was like an out-of-scale paint-by-numbers and they just had to stay between the lines, but maybe, she supposed it was possible, it was a special talent and they painted from a vision like Michelangelo.

Louise didn't know how long she'd been watching before she realized what it was she was seeing. The knowledge was just suddenly there in her mind as though she'd known it all along or had grasped a concept spatially, without linear steps. She couldn't remember the instant of recognition. It was like a play within a play, or nesting dolls, diminishing degrees of reality as cinema is to life. A shock to realize after watching — for how long? — that the words that were being painted across the billboard sky advertised M.'s movie. This was the omen the morning promised, Louise thought, but portending what? It was as though she hadn't awakened at all but dreamed on in obscure symbols. It seemed neat, designed especially for her, a grand gesture like a declaration made in skywriting, but one she couldn't interpret.

Louise was bemused and unable to concentrate on the newspaper. She kept looking up from the page to monitor the progress of the painters. She thought about telephoning M. "Guess what I can see from here?" It was the normal thing to do in the circumstances, or would be the normal thing if their relationship were different. But when she imagined what she'd say it sounded trite to her own ears, an exaggeration of a minor coincidence like a Valley girl's dramatics. It was the beleaguered and the powerless, the children of the planet, who sought to invest chaos and chance with a pattern of intent which could be divined through occult sciences like phrenology or astrology or palmistry. There wasn't any hidden message in a glimpse of a billboard advertising a friend's movie. She'd made less of larger coincidences in other circumstances when she'd had less yearning for meaning.

There was comfort in imagining that life was a journey for which you had a destination and a set course but no map, a sojourn into uncharted territory. But really, there was no future, you were sailing into nothing and there was no one at the helm. They were all poised on the lip of the present like lemmings at the edge of the world. The future was only a concept to explain the mystery that lay beyond the expanding edge of the universe, and did not exist at all. There was only the present instant.

Louise would have been happy to never leave the Château. She could live in the room and on the balcony and in the salmon tiled bathroom, never once get dressed. Watch from the bed when a wind came up and flapped the French door and lightning touched the cypress and the air smelled of hot pitch. She'd order up for every meal, a legendary nut case as the years wore on, stories passed down through generations of staff. Like Delta Dawn, paralyzed, frozen in time while the world advanced without her. She might talk gibberish or strew flowers from the balcony onto the roofs of departing cars, gardenia petals like fragrant snow.

But there were still threads of sanity she couldn't sever lashing her like Gulliver to reality. Practical considerations entered. The rental car downstairs in the garage with guns in the trunk, an airline ticket home. The kids and the cat. Madness was a kind of regression, and to come back from it she'd have to pass through here again. It might be better to catch herself, brace where she was, resist the slide and claw back up. She checked out of the Château.

seventeen

SOMETHING HAD SHIFTED, though, a tilt altering her course. She pictured dire events. M.'s plane going down. An accident in the canyon or on the autostrada, and how would she ever know? He was a wild driver, not defensive at all. Or a heart attack. She wouldn't be notified. No one would know to call. She seldom saw the trade papers. Months could go by. She'd assume he'd tired of her.

And at the same time he was before her more than ever. They weren't yet done editing, but there was a trailer playing the theaters, an early warning for a summer release, and a profile in one of the monthly film journals.

Louise tried to think of other things.

At the lake, standing on the shore — impossible to tell without field glasses which boats her sons were rowing in — Louise heard her husband call her name. She turned around, a smile emerging from some archive of automatic response. For a moment she was lit up with an impulse of affection and delight before her guard dropped into place like a visor. She wondered if he felt the same bleak chill like a sudden cloud, a change in the weather.

Looking at him, an affable moon-faced man, she had no idea who he was, though once she was able to predict everything he'd say or do. It was as though he'd been in remission, away somewhere during their marriage, leaving an effigy in his place like Charlie McCarthy sitting on her knee, vacant unless animated by her. She wondered if he was back, at home in there, or was now someone else's creation. For a while, when he was married a second time, he'd worn painted ties and silk shirts, wide pleated pants breaking over Italian loafers, as though illustrating a previously censored flamboyance or his new wife's idea of him. Now in his third marriage, Louise wondered if he was in another disguise or if this stranger was really him, if a more embracing woman had encouraged him to inhabit his own person.

Louise had no idea what was going to come out of his mouth. They looked at each other. "How're you doing?" was what he finally said.

She laughed. That was all? "Fine," she said, and waited, refusing any help. Foolish, perhaps, to inhibit good will, but there was an unmapped continent of betrayal between them. But habits took an eternity to break. For so long after their divorce, when most of what they had to say to each other was in rancorous exchanges over support or visitation, she'd hear herself calling him Honey.

The boats were coming in, arrows on the water. Louise could tell her sons now by the color of the shirts and could hear the coxswains yell. Elliot cheered through cupped hands, bellowing encouragement. The boats shot across the finish, then slowed and drifted like water bugs.

Louise looked at her former husband — her mother's legacy to say former, never ex, a matter of taste lost on the rest of the world. He shuffled in his aw-shucks manner and nodded toward the dock. "Are you coming?"

"In a moment," she said, and watched as he walked away and was joined by his wife, emerging from the crowd like a tentacle attaching herself to him. He would be in the way on the dock, a golden retriever wagging all over in pride and enthusiasm, ducking oars, trying to reach the right kids as the boats came out of the water, snapping photos. Louise hung back, but caught her younger son's eye, checking for her.

People were uncomfortable around her, the other parents, couples, tongue-tied as though there'd been a death or illness

162

and they didn't know the protocol. Did you offer condolences or skirt the subject, talk commonplaces? She was an ominous reminder of misfortune and they imagined that in her presence their own unions were in jeopardy but had no idea what to do about it. They hemmed and shifted and escaped as soon as possible. Louise felt like another species.

She went home alone. She could imagine how she looked to other eyes if anyone watched her climbing the hill toward where she'd parked the car, a solitary figure with her hands jammed into the pockets of her combat jacket.

Then, in a paradoxical marketing strategy, M.'s movie opened in Seattle at the end of the film festival. Not a festival sort of a picture, but a parabolically glamorous finale after weeks of experimental noir. What all the hopefuls might one day come to. Louise went alone, sat on the aisle, and left before the credits rolled. She had no impression of the movie. She'd have to see it again.

Her timing was bad. M. was in the lobby with his wife, the publicist, and a local critic Louise knew. They turned and looked up as she pushed through the door, interested to read reactions but not expecting her. She was frozen for a moment, holding M.'s eyes, but then there were people behind her, pushing past, and she let herself be swept up and carried out.

A limousine waited at the curb to bear him away to the airport or a reception somewhere, dinner. Whatever festivities were planned. Doors closed to her.

When the phone rang late in the night Louise didn't answer. The hardest thing she'd ever done. She longed to hear his voice, to plan to meet. He'd stay an extra day, let his wife go home ahead.

Louise was alone in the house. The boys were with their father, his six weeks of summer. She got out of bed and stood in the darkness at the window looking out, distancing herself from the bedside phone, the temptation to snatch it up. Four interminable rings before the answering machine in her study downstairs picked up.

In the morning she put her mother's ashes and her grand-mother's in the trunk of the Towncar. It was over now, she thought, severed finally somehow by her own will. Now she'd lay it all to rest. Bury M. and her mother both. Somewhere in Montana she'd cut north toward Edmonton.

Louise slipped behind the wheel and headed east without listening to the message M. had left.

EPILOGUE

LATE IN THE afternoon of the second day she was stopped by a paving crew that had two-way traffic halted on the secondary highway she was traveling. She could have stayed on the interstates, but had wanted to drive through Two Dot and White Sulfur Springs on her way north.

She turned off the engine and got out to await the return of the pilot car. The flagger was idle. There was no one else, no other traffic lining up. The sun was hot and the wind smelled of tar. In the west thunderheads were spilling over the rim of the Little Belts. She was in no hurry. She leaned against the Lincoln, watching the men and equipment through the heat shimmer while she waited.

A pickup came traveling up through the barrow pit from the opposite direction and stopped near all the activity. A boss, she imagined as she watched him get out, not as dirty as the crew and wearing a shirt. He looked her way as he closed the door and she didn't know which she saw first — his face or the name painted on the side of the pickup. It said Gallegos Brothers and he looked like he had, like she'd always imagined him, hardly older, though it had been more than twenty years.

She had the advantage because of the name, but though people had come up to him and someone was shouting something to him over the noise of the equipment, even so he was still looking at her.

Time stopped while they stared.

She put her hands to her face and turned away. When she turned back he was walking toward her.